Vision of Death

**
*

The golden man appeared, naked and silent as a shadow, at the far end of a row of lockers. Blood still flowed freely from his nose and mouth, but he gave no indication that he was in pain. He stared for a few moments at Veil, who was sitting on a long wooden bench, gagging and coughing as he slumped over a blue canvas bag.

"You should have done as I asked," the golden man said, lisping slightly as his tongue passed over the space where his front teeth had been. "You hurt me, and now I'm going to hurt you before I kill you. In the end it will still look as though you drowned."

Suddenly Veil straightened. There was a flash of movement as his hand came out of the bag and he hurled a set of heavy ankle weights at the assassin's head. The golden man calmly reached out and plucked the leather-and-lead missile from the air. The golden man smiled with contempt, then shrugged and started to toss the weights to one side. In that instant of wasted motion and flickering concentration, Veil threw the bench.

VEIL

GEORGE C. CHESBRO

THE MYSTERIOUS PRESS

New York • London

MYSTERIOUS PRESS EDITION

Copyright © 1986 by George C. Chesbro

Mysterious Press books are published in association with
Warner Books, Inc.
666 Fifth Avenue
New York, N.Y. 10103
A Warner Communications Company

Printed in the United States of America

Originally published in hardcover by The Mysterious Press.
First Mysterious Press Paperback Printing: September, 1987

10 9 8 7 6 5 4 3 2 1

For my parents,
George W. and Maxine S. Chesbro

Questar Press Paperback Printing September, 1987

Chapter 1

Veil dreams.

Vivid dreaming is his gift and affliction, the lash of memory and a guide to justice, a mystery and sometimes the key to mystery, prod to violence and maker of peace, an invitation to madness and the fountainhead of his power as an artist.

Chapter 2

Dinner had been in the grand manner, French cuisine expertly prepared and graciously served in an elegant setting that provided a feast for all the senses. Now Veil Kendry stood on the great stone balcony outside the dining hall, sipping cognac as he watched moonlight splinter and dance on the shimmering surface of the sea hundreds of feet below him. Somewhere at the botton of the night, seals barked.

Kendry was impressed. The Institute for Human Studies was spread over the top third of a mountain in California's Big Sur, fifty miles from Monterey. The Institute was concerned solely with what its brochure described as "extreme people." Its staff probed the limits of human accomplishment and endurance through the exhaustive physical and psychological analysis of uniquely gifted individuals who came to the Institute by highly prized invitation. The equipment in the Institute's many laboratories was state-of-the-art, its approach relentlessly multidisciplinary, and its staff represented the elite in dozens of fields. Nobel laureates felt privileged to be invited to lecture or perform research at the Institute.

Veil turned around and studied the others who had joined him on the balcony. The world chess champion, a Russian, was chatting amiably, through an Institute interpreter, with an eleven-year-old Israeli violin virtuoso. In a dark corner the National Football League's all-time leading pass receiver was engaged in quiet conversation with one of the attractive hostesses who had presided over the dinner. An Australian bushman, a man who could trek for three days through open desert on a cup of water, stood stiff and obviously uncomfortable as he fingered a lumpy totem made of ostrich skin.

Veil was definitely odd man out at this gathering, and he couldn't understand why he had received an invitation to spend a month at the Institute. As far as he knew, all of the other guests possessed strikingly unusual talents. All he did was paint pictures, and he was not exactly reeling under the burden of success. Indeed, he was surprised that someone like Jonathan Pilgrim had even heard of him; the critics were once again genuflecting before minimalist art, and he hadn't sold a painting in months. He didn't have enough money in the bank to buy even one of the expensive bottles of wine that had flowed so copiously during the meal.

Veil knew that he was, to be sure, an "extreme person"— but Pilgrim and his research staff could not be aware of it without knowing the extent and consequences of his brain damage, or somehow gaining access to one of the nation's most carefully guarded military secrets. Both events were highly improbable.

"Mr. Kendry?"

Veil turned to his left to discover the founder and executive director of the Institute standing beside him. Jonathan Pilgrim, like most of the astronauts, stood just under six feet— Veil's height. Pilgrim, in his mid-forties, was lean and muscular. Thick, unruly brown hair was creased by a scar that radiated to his right temple from the lacy mapwork of nerveless, ruined tissue that covered his right cheek. His left eye was green, and a beige patch covered the empty socket where the right eye had been. A simple stainless-steel hook protruded from the left sleeve of his dinner jacket. Scars, hook, and patch notwithstanding, Veil thought, Pilgrim looked remarkably fit for a man who'd returned from the land of the dead.

"Colonel Pilgrim," he said, gripping the man's outstretched hand.

"I'm sorry I missed you at dinner, Kendry. Welcome to the Institute."

"I feel very privileged to have been invited, Colonel."

"Forget the 'Colonel' crap, Veil. My name's Jonathan."

Veil nodded. "All right, Jonathan," he replied evenly.

"I'm only 'Colonel' to some of the fools I have to cater to around here."

"Some fools."

Pilgrim lit a cigar, puffed thoughtfully, then blew a thin stream of smoke out into the eddies of wind blowing across the surface of the sea. "Being highly gifted isn't all it's cracked up to be. Two sessions ago we had a man here whom a lot of people thought might be the smartest person on earth. He went right off the charts on all the standard intelligence tests, so we had to have an IBM mainframe design one that wouldn't put him to sleep. The night before he was to take the test, a hostess caught him stuffing silverware into the beaded purse he carried."

Veil smiled. "What did you do with him?"

"I threw the thieving son of a bitch out on his fat ass, naturally."

Veil's smile grew broader. He felt a strange bond of kinship with this gregarious, unassuming man who was one of the few people he admired and respected without reservation.

"Rare gifts sometimes carry a steep price tag," Pilgrim continued easily. "You'll find a lot of people here tonight with elevators that don't go all the way to the top."

"At the risk of branding myself, how do you know that my elevator goes all the way to the top?"

"Good instincts," Pilgrim replied, his one eye glinting with amusement. "Veil. I like that. Family name?"

"Not exactly. I was born with a brain infection, and a caul, and I wasn't expected to live more than two or three hours. My folks had a mystical bent, and I guess they figured that a little metaphysics at the christening couldn't hurt."

"It looks to me like they may have been on to something."

"Could be."

"What about you? Do you have a mystical bent?"

"I believe in gravity, mathematics, and mystery."

"What do you use for an ethical system?"

"Do unto others as you would have them do unto you, and watch out for the bad guys."

Pilgrim laughed. "Nobody's going to accuse you of not being forthcoming."

"I read the Institute contract before I signed it," Veil replied with a shrug. "I get a month of fresh air, great scenery, and legendary meals in exchange for letting you turn me inside out."

"True. We do want to extract as much information as we can from your mind and body, but that doesn't mean that you have to chat us up at cocktail parties."

"The pleasure of talking to you and answering your questions is mine, Jonathan. The fact is that I don't understand why you invited me here in the first place."

"Success isn't the criterion for being asked to come here; uniqueness is. Your work is unique."

"That and a dollar will buy me a cup of coffee in Times Square. But thank you, Jonathan."

"You've had your intake interview with Henry—Dr. Ibber. You'll be talking to a lot of other people from a number of different disciplines. You'll have all sorts of machines beeping in your face, be goosed in more holes than you know you have, and undergo hypnosis. If you have no objections, we may even try a few tricks with sensory deprivation."

Veil suppressed harsh, sour laughter that he was certain would be misunderstood. He had endured far worse than anything they could do to him here, had seen others endure

6

far worse. He felt a chill. "I can understand running tests like that on an athlete," he said quietly, "but I'm not sure I see the point with a painter."

"Why? Because the creative act is, and always shall remain, a mystery?"

"Something like that."

"Well, you could be right. In any case, we'll be taking a long, hard look at the right hemisphere of your brain."

"I'll have no objections to anything you want to do with me, Jonathan. It all sounds very interesting."

"Good. Where did you learn to paint?"

"I'm still learning to paint."

"Self-taught?"

Veil nodded.

"Critics call your work 'dream painting.' Is that how you think of it?"

"Not really. Most of my paintings are based on the colors and textures of dreams, but I never think of my work in terms of a label."

"Still," Pilgrim said in what seemed to Veil a curiously flat, neutral tone, "you must have exceptionally vivid dreams."

Veil hesitated before this probe into the deepest part of his being. Then he reminded himself of the commitment he had made, and he decided he would not cheat Pilgrim or his Institute. "I do," he said after a pause. "The cause is organic. The infection I mentioned caused some brain damage. In effect, it tore away the protective psychic membrane everyone else has between the conscious and subconscious. For me, dreams and reality are experienced in pretty much the same way—although I did finally learn to tell when I'm dreaming." He paused again, smiled thinly. "Before I picked up that particular skill, dreaming caused me one or two problems."

"Jesus, I would think so," Pilgrim said in a hushed tone that was just above a whisper. "You must know one or two things about terror."

Jonathan Pilgrim was a very perceptive and wise man, Veil thought. His reply was a shrug.

"Have you ever had a CAT scan?"

"A number of times. I can have the results sent here, if you'd like."

"We'd prefer to do our own."

"You'll find lesions on the pons and hippocampus, as well as some minimal synaptic damage."

Pilgrim nodded absently as he blew a smoke ring that was immediately swallowed by the wind. Veil had the distinct impression that Pilgrim badly wanted to pursue this line of questioning, but for some reason the director of the Institute for Human Studies now chose to remain silent.

"If you don't mind, there are a few things I'd like to ask you," Veil continued at last.

Pilgrim casually tossed the butt of his cigar over the balcony's marble railing. "Ask away, Veil."

"Where did you get the idea for the Institute?"

Pilgrim laughed softly. "In space, of course. Where else? Space is a bit spooky, and out there the brilliant insight came to me that we're just a bit spooky ourselves. I thought it would be nice if, one day, all the best people, ideas, and research connected with human studies could be brought together in one facility. After the accident, I had the time to put it together."

"How do you fund it?"

"We publish a number of scientific journals, as well as a hefty psychobiological newsletter that a few industries and government agencies find useful, and which they don't mind paying a lot of money for. We do recombinant DNA research, and we hold better than two hundred patents in the field. We do some contract work for corporations. We have an excellent sports-medicine complex, and most of the pro teams use us on occasion to evaluate prospects. We generate some money from books and lecture fees, and once in a while some film studio will spring with a lot of cash for the privilege of using the grounds for location shooting. I suppose we get more than our share of bequests, foundation money, and what's left of the government grants. For the rest, I go out and tap-dance."

"I'm very impressed, Jonathan. You've done one hell of a job."

"Well, I'm happy you could accept our invitation."

"What happens next?"

"Psychological tests. I've arranged an appointment for you with one of our psychologists, Dr. Solow, at ten in the morning. Okay?"

"Sure."

"You'll find a golf cart parked outside your cottage, and a map of the grounds on the desk inside. The psychometric labs are in the C building. If you don't feel like chauffeuring yourself, I'll have someone on the staff pick you up."

"I'll drive myself."

"When you're not scheduled for tests, feel free to wander around. Some of the things we do may interest you."

"I know they will."

"Is there anything you need?"

"A place to work out, if you have one."

"There's a fully equipped gym in the basement of F building. It has a weight room with a Nautilus, a pool, steam room, and sauna. If that doesn't suit you, you can always jog around the complex."

"Terrific."

"Anything else?"

"No. Thank you."

"Then I'll be saying good night."

"Good night, Jonathan."

Chapter 3

Veil dreams.

The seven Hmong tribesmen who've escorted him to the meeting site form a semicircle to protect his flanks and back. The Hmongs' automatic rifles are held at the ready as they peer into the surrounding jungle and listen intently for sounds of the enemy. Veil, his M-60 machine gun slung around his bare torso, stands in the middle of the clearing. The humid air is fetid with the smell of rotting vegetation and the human excrement used by the Laotians as fertilizer.

Shortly after three o'clock the helicopter appears in the southwest. Flying at a high altitude to avoid mortar and small-arms fire, the helicopter first appears as a mere speck in the azure sky. The *whop-whop-whop* of its rotors grows steadily louder as it approaches, then drops at a sharp angle from the sky to hover a foot off the ground at the far end of the clearing. Colonel Bean, Orville Madison, and an ARVN major jump from the Huey, crouch beneath the rotors, and hurry toward Veil. Bean and the South Vietnamese are dressed in fatigues; the sluglike Madison wears a tan summer suit stained with sweat at the crotch and from armpit to waist on both sides. Veil knows that Madison's presence is a bad omen. In addition to being an army officer, Veil is a Central Intelligence Agency operative; here, in the midst of an agency-run secret war in Laos, it is Madison who is Veil's superior, not Bean. A decision has been made which he is not going to like, Veil thinks, and Madison is here to make it stick.

"Captain Kendry, I presume," Colonel Bean says, gesturing derisively at the half-naked men who have now moved to surround them all. He very much dislikes Veil, fears him even more.

"You picked a bad time to call a meeting," Veil says in a flat tone. He addresses his controller, ignoring Bean and the ARVN major. "We had visitors last night, and they left a mess. They may still be around. I imagine the Pathet Lao would dearly love to capture two American officers, one South Vietnamese officer, and a CIA field officer inside their borders. After they take our pictures and tape our confessions, they'll have us all eating our balls for dinner. I'm sure they've been tracking that damn helicopter since you crossed the line. If you wanted to see me, you should have walked in."

Bean tenses and removes the safety on his rifle, while Madison glances nervously around him. Only the South Vietnamese does not react. He is a tall man, over six feet, and rangy. His face is as impassive as the Hmong who guard them. If any emotion shows in his almond-colored eyes, it is vague amusement.

"No time for that, Kendry," Madison says tersely. "I've got orders to make certain you hang on to your balls. You're coming out with us. Today."

"Bullshit," Veil replies without emotion.

Bean flushes and slaps the stock of his rifle. "Damn it, Kendry, you watch your mouth!"

Madison holds up a pudgy hand, silencing the other

American. "Now, Colonel, just take it easy," he says, looking directly at Veil. "Everyone knows that Captain Kendry has bad table manners, but he also happens to be a bona fide hero—and that's what's been requisitioned."

Veil spits contemptuously, barely missing the CIA controller's foot. Bean clenches his jaw and looks away; the ARVN major stifles a yawn; Madison pretends not to notice. "Stop trying to blow smoke up my ass and get to the point," Veil snaps at Madison. He is aware of the core of steel beneath Madison's fat, but he has a very bad feeling about this situation and knows that he must constantly confront Madison in an effort to avoid being manipulated. He knows that he will lose in the end if the controller seriously wants something, but still feels compelled to struggle; Madison is always groping for the throat of the soul. "We've already been standing out here in the open too long. What the hell are you people doing here?"

"This meeting is about winning the war," Madison replies in a soft, dangerous tone. He does not take his eyes from Veil's face. "A whole continent of gooks can't beat us, but American families with their sons coming home in body bags or running off to Canada can. That's what's happening back home, Captain; we're losing support, and if we lose enough support, we'll lose the war. You didn't run off to Canada, and I'm here to make damn sure you don't go home in a body bag. You've made quite a name for yourself, both back in 'Nam and during the time you've spent here—although God knows how so many people seem to know you're in Laos. It doesn't make any difference; we'll find a way to use it. Charlie and the Pathet Lao call you 'Yellow Beast,' Kendry. There's a big price on your head. Did you know that?"

"Madison—"

"What America needs is a Sergeant York or Audie Murphy for *this* war, Kendry. You're it. You're it, not because I say so or the Army says so, but because some important congressmen and the President of the United States say so. As a matter of fact, the President is shining up a Congressional Medal of

Honor to go with all the silver, bronze, and ribbon you have. You're going to be our point man at home, the spokesman for this war. The PR machinery is being cranked up right at this moment. That good-looking face of yours is going to be in newspapers and on magazine covers; it's going to be on U.S. Army recruiting posters, and probably in comic books. You're going to be the subject of television documentaries. A very good writer is whipping up a screenplay for a feature film about you, and John Wayne has agreed to produce as well as lend his name to the project. You're going to be traveling from one end of the country to the other, up and down and back again. You, Captain Kendry, are going to put on one hell of a show. End of discussion."

Veil is stunned into silence. His mouth is dry. The air in his lungs feels thick and heavy, like that of some alien planet.

"You asked for it straight, Captain," Madison continues, "so that's how I gave it to you. You're going to Tokyo for six weeks for a little R and R and some very specific instructions on how you're going to handle this new assignment. Needless to say, the poor innocents who dreamed up this stunt can't begin to appreciate what a truly insane, insubordinate son of a bitch you really are."

Veil shakes his head. He feels shamed. "Don't do this to me, Madison," he says quietly. "I'm a soldier, not a performer."

"After Tokyo you'll come back to Saigon for appropriate awards ceremonies jointly conducted by us and the South Vietnamese. Then you're off to the States." Madison pauses, nods toward the impassive Vietnamese. "This is Major Po. He's your replacement here. I want you to introduce him to your people, and then we're getting the hell out—"

This is an exceptionally unpleasant dream, which Veil has not experienced for years. Since learning how to control them, he has trusted his dreams, for they have often proved useful to him. But he cannot understand why he should be dreaming of

14

Southeast Asia and events that had occurred so many years in the past. Unable to see any connection between where he was then and where he is now, Veil rolls out of the dream and segues into deep, restful sleep.

Chapter 4

Veil completed a third set of bench presses and eased the weights down onto the holding rack above his head. He pushed back his long, sweat-soaked blond hair, sat up, and studied himself in the wall mirror as he waited for his pulse to normalize and the satisfying ache in his muscles to ease. His pale blue, gold-flecked eyes narrowed as he appraised what he saw. There were scars, of course, including a puckered mound the size of a baby's fist on his right side where a lance of twisted metal had skewered him and collapsed a lung, but his body was solid; the muscles in his stomach, chest, arms, and legs clearly articulated.

Satisfied with his workout, Veil rose and walked to the showers, passing through a cloud of musky-smelling mist that was leaking from the half-open door of the steam room. He shuddered under an ice-cold needle spray for a few seconds, then padded down a narrow, tiled corridor leading to the pool.

He knifed cleanly into the still, blue water and swam the twenty-five-meter length of the pool under water, pulling rhythmically with his arms and using a powerful scissors kick. As he reached the shallow end he had the abrupt, alarming sensation that someone was stuffing a flannel rag down his throat. He surfaced and began to cough violently.

Finally the racking spasm passed. Puzzled, Veil took a series of deep breaths as he rubbed his sore chest and swallowed repeatedly. Feeling no lingering ill effects, he pushed off the wall and lazily backstroked toward the deep end. Without warning he began to cough again, and he barely managed to keep from swallowing water. There was a bitter medicinal taste at the back of his throat, and he felt as if he had been gassed.

The steam room, Veil thought.

He heard the familiar sound of soft, distant chimes in his head, and knew he was in terrible danger.

He twisted around in the water in time to see a golden shape angling up toward him from the bottom of the pool. He had heard no sound—no closing doors in the locker room, no smack of feet on tile, no splash as the man had entered the water.

Veil rolled to his left and jackknifed beneath the surface. A hand grabbed for his ankle, missed, caught hold of his left wrist, and yanked. Fighting against dizziness and a swelling pressure behind his eyes, he relaxed and allowed himself to be pulled toward the bottom of the pool. The fingers on his wrist were very strong, powerful enough to snap bone. He knew that he had to control his gag reflex, for he would drown if he coughed. That was what the man wanted; he had been gassed just enough to make him an easy target.

Veil reached across his body and wrapped the fingers of his right hand around the man's wrist. He pivoted a quarter turn, brought his knees up to his chest, and kicked under the man's extended arm into his rib cage. Despite the fact that Veil's strength was rapidly failing, the blow landed with enough force to break the wristlock and drive the man away. There was a gurgle of surprise, accompanied by a burst of bubbles

18

that shimmered with a pink glow in his drug-clouded field of vision.

Veil swept his arms up over his head, driving himself down hard to a squatting position on the bottom. He immediately pushed off, extending his arms over his head and angling toward the side of the pool. He broke the surface just inches from the edge, slapped his palms on the deck, and pulled. His momentum carried him cleanly out of the water. He swayed with dizziness, coughing and gasping for breath, but managed to stay on his feet.

He had to get into the locker room, had to get to his gym bag.

There was an explosion of water four feet to his right as the yellow-haired, deeply tanned man burst out of the water like a missile launched from a submarine. The golden man landed light as a cat on the deck, then immediately dropped on his hands and executed a gymnast's leg sweep in an attempt to cut Veil's legs out from under him.

Veil hopped over the scythe of the man's legs, then dove toward the center of the pool. He entered the water at a sharp angle and, wincing at the sick pain in his head, immediately reversed his direction, crabbing down and back. The golden man landed in the water and shot past overhead. Veil turned, pulled to the surface, and again hopped up on the deck. He grabbed a long-poled skimming net from a rack on the wall, spun around, and crouched, ready to jab with the pole's blunt end. His muscles felt rubbery.

The golden man was treading water easily in the center of the pool, long yellow hair floating around his shoulders. There was surprise and respect in the dark brown eyes that studied Veil. "Don't resist," he said in a flat voice. "It won't do you any good. I won't hurt you if you don't force me to. You won't feel anything."

American, Veil thought. Home-grown talent. He judged him to be in his mid-twenties. It was all Veil could do to draw a breath, and the golden man wasn't even breathing hard. "My dentist used to say things like that," Veil replied in a voice that sounded like it came from an echo chamber inside his head. "I think I'll decline your offer and just wait here until somebody shows up."

"The doors are locked. Nobody's coming in, and you're not walking out."

"Talk is cheap, my young friend. What else do you have to show me besides your vocabulary?"

"I heard you used to be quite the martial artist, Kendry. Well, you're not anywhere near top stuff now. You're past it. Even without that shit in you, you'd be no match for me. Accept my offer."

"If you think you're so goddam good, why don't you wait for me on the other side of the pool? As soon as I stop seeing two of you, I'll see if I can't make you work up a sweat."

"Don't take me for a fool, Kendry. I was just stating a fact, not issuing a challenge. This is just business."

"You're Madison's man, right? How is that fat, sadistic bastard?"

The golden man did not answer.

"Why the hell pick this place to come after me?" Veil continued. "What was wrong with New York?"

The golden man's response this time was a faint smile as, head up and eyes fixed on the end of the skimming net pole, he began to glide slowly toward Veil.

He waited until the man was a few feet closer, then hurled the pole at his head. The golden man casually knocked the pole away with the side of a thickly callused hand. Veil launched himself into the air. He soared over the golden man's head, landed flat on his stomach and chest in a racing dive, and sprinted toward the opposite side.

Now he was exactly where the assassin wanted him, Veil thought, in the water. But swimming across the pool was the most direct route to the locker room, and that was where he had to go. The time he had already gained seemed to be working to his advantage, for he no longer had the urge to gag and cough. The drug was passing out of his system. He felt better but nowhere near well enough to turn and fight. He needed still more time.

Feigning only slightly more exhaustion than he actually

felt, Veil slowed as he approached the side and listened carefully to the sound of the golden man thrashing through the water after him. He gripped the edge, made a motion as if he were going to haul himself out of the water, then flipped over on his back, cocked his right leg, and kicked out at the golden man's face. The assassin managed to partially block the kick, but a popping sound and a rush of blood told Veil that, at the least, the man's nose was broken.

The assassin grabbed for Veil's ankle, but Veil was already out of the water and staggering into the locker room.

More than a minute passed. Then the golden man appeared, naked and silent as a shadow, at the far end of a row of lockers. Blood still flowed freely from his nose and mouth, but he gave no indication that he was in pain. He stared for a few moments at Veil, who was sitting on a long wooden bench, gagging and coughing as he slumped over a blue canvas gym bag.

"You should have done as I asked," the golden man said, lisping slightly as his tongue passed over the space where his front teeth had been. "You hurt me, and now I'm going to hurt you before I kill you. In the end it will still look as though you drowned."

Suddenly Veil straightened. There was a flash of movement as his hand came out of the bag and he hurled a set of heavy ankle weights at the assassin's head. Displaying incredible reflexes, depth perception, and nerve, the golden man calmly reached out and plucked the leather-and-lead missile from the air. The golden man smiled with contempt, then shrugged and started to toss the weights to one side. In that instant of wasted motion and flickering concentration, Veil threw the bench. The golden man was able to sidestep the flying bench, but by then Veil was in on him.

" I didn't like it much when that man took it."

Chapter 5

Where did you learn to use your hands like that, Kendry?"

"I don't know what you mean, Lieutenant."

"You tore away a man's throat with your bare hands."

"That's ridiculous, Lieutenant. I don't even have long fingernails."

"Don't be a fucking wise-ass! You did it! I want to know where you *learned* how to do it."

"I pushed him away from me," Veil replied quietly. "He tripped and caught his throat on the sharp edge of the locker. It was a freak accident."

"Do you expect me to believe that story?"

"It's true."

"You're not going to like it much if I decide to book you on a murder charge."

"I didn't like it much when that man tried to rob me."

23

"Tell me again what happened."

"I'd worked out in the weight room and taken a swim. I was getting dressed when this man came up. He swung those ankle weights in my face and demanded my wallet."

"The man was naked, Kendry. Have you ever heard of a naked mugger?"

"Come on, Lieutenant. This happened in a locker room. Obviously, the man was on his way to take a swim. He noticed me coming out of the pool and figured I was an easy mark."

"You don't look like an easy mark to me, Kendry. As a matter of fact, you look pretty damn solid."

"He had the weights. He said he was going to smash in my face if I didn't give him the wallet."

The man questioning him snorted with disgust and looked away. Veil relaxed slightly and glanced around the room. There were three men with him in the small reception area outside the director's office. His interrogator had been introduced to him as Lieutenant Parker. Parker was a lean, hard man whom Veil judged to be in his mid-fifties. His close-cropped, iron-gray hair matched the color of his eyes. He kept toying with a pencil and yellow pad set squarely in front of him on a secretary's desk, but he had yet to write anything down. There was an almost palpable air of suspicion and disbelief about the man, but he did not seem able to mount a sustained verbal attack. It struck him that Parker badly wanted to pursue a different line of questioning, but for some reason felt constrained from doing so.

Dr. Henry Ibber, the Institute's chief investigator and the man who had conducted Veil's intake interview, stood leaning against the wall just behind Parker. Dressed in brown slacks, black turtleneck, and rust-colored tweed jacket, the physician seemed almost as nervous as Parker. Prematurely bald with a droopy mustache that framed thin lips, Ibber kept shifting his weight from one foot to the other as his dark eyes darted about the room. Veil judged the man to be in his early thirties, and tougher than he looked.

Only Jonathan Pilgrim seemed at ease. The director was slouched in a leather armchair at the far corner of the room, his booted feet propped up on a coffee table. He was smoking one of his thin cigars and staring up through a haze of blue-gray smoke at the ceiling. Pilgrim's demeanor seemed to Veil somewhat bizarre under the circumstances. Like a magnet, the slouched figure kept drawing annoyed glances from Parker.

"Am I boring you, Colonel?!" Parker snapped. "A man's been killed!"

"That's certainly true," Pilgrim replied in a mild tone, "and I'm certainly glad it wasn't Mr. Kendry." Pilgrim slowly swung his feet to the floor, straightened up, and ground out his cigar. When he looked up, there was a hard glint in his eye. "I think you're being overzealous, Lieutenant. Dr. Ibber and I have told you that the dead man was one of our cooks. When they're off duty, our staff enjoys the privilege of using the recreational facilities. It looks like we hired ourselves a bad apple. It happens. Also, it does seem unlikely that an artist could tear out another man's throat with his bare hands, doesn't it? So, why the hassle?"

Blood rushed to Parker's face, and for a moment Veil thought the man would pound the desk. They gray-haired man swallowed hard, brought himself back under control. "All right, Kendry," he said at last, his voice gravelly with frustration.

Veil met the other man's hostile gaze. "Meaning?"

"Meaning that I know where to find you if I have any more questions."

Pilgrim abruptly rose to his feet. "Sorry for the trouble, Kendry. Are you certain you feel all right?"

Veil nodded.

"Good luck to you," Pilgrim continued brusquely as he walked across the reception area, opened a door, and disappeared into his office.

The director had left the door to his office open, and Veil had a clear, if restricted, view of the interior. A modern glass-

and-steel desk was visible, and on the wall behind the desk a map on a spring roller had been pulled down. The map appeared to be a larger version of the one printed in the Institute brochures, except that it included two huge gray areas, each at least half again the size of the "official" compound. One area was on the northern face of an adjacent mountain, and the second was at the eastern end of the valley running between the two mountains. Neither area was labeled.

A moment later his view was blocked as Henry Ibber moved quickly across the room and pushed the door shut. Parker, red-faced and seething, rose and walked stiffly out the door. Veil glanced inquiringly at Ibber, who seemed embarrassed.

"Kendry," Ibber said tightly, "this is an uncomfortable situation for both the Colonel and me."

Veil smiled thinly. "I think I'm about to have my invitation withdrawn."

Ibber took a deep breath as he thrust his hands into the pockets of his tweed jacket. "Even though you seem perfectly collected, a traumatic experience like the one you've just had can't help but leave deep and disturbing emotional overtones which may be with you for some time. Under the circumstances, it would be impossible for us to properly conduct the kinds of tests we'd planned for you. I hope you understand."

Veil gave a slight shrug, rose to his feet. "Sure. Keeping me around might cause some deep and disturbing emotional overtones in the other guests, not to mention your ex-cook's buddies."

"That isn't the point, Mr. Kendry, I assure you. In fact, we'd like to reschedule you for another session, perhaps in six months or so."

"I'll look forward to it."

Ibber smiled uncertainly. "There's no need for you to leave right away. Why don't you stay the night? In the morning someone can take you to the airport in the helicopter. We'll drop off your rented car."

"I think not. I'd just as soon fly out tonight, and I prefer to drive myself."

"As you wish."

Veil stared hard at the other man for a few moments, until Ibber averted his eyes. "I know my way to the garage," he said as he headed for the door. "Nice meeting you, Ibber. Tell the Colonel I said good-bye."

Barry noticed that he was surrounded by a small
depression across the road from a highly figured hol...

Chapter 6

Veil stopped for an hour along a barren stretch of coast. Satisfied that he wasn't being followed, he drove on to the outskirts of Monterey and checked into a dingy, third-rate motel under an assumed name. He stayed in his room the remainder of the day, went out to eat an early dinner, then went to bed after leaving a request for a ten P.M. wake-up call. By one in the morning he was back at the base of the Institute's mountain. He drove his car off the side of the road into a copse of fir trees a half mile from the entrance to the underground parking area, then walked back.

The service road leading up to the compound at the top of the mountain was located twenty yards to the right of the closed-down funicular. Veil stepped over the chain blocking the entrance to the road and started up.

Forty minutes later he was hunched down in a shallow depression across the road from a brightly lighted helicopter pad. There was a small guardhouse inside a high chain-link fence topped with barbed wire. Veil went a hundred yards beyond the pad and guardhouse, then crossed the road to the fence. He had not seen any transformers on the way up, and so he assumed that the fence was not electrified. He checked to be certain that the 38-caliber snub-nose he had retrieved from the car was secure in his waistband, against his spine, then removed his garrison belt from his jeans and gripped it between his teeth as he easily climbed the fence. At the top he wrapped the belt around the palm of his right hand and pressed down on the strands of barbed wire. He swung through the V of the wire and dropped down on the other side, rolling to absorb the shock of his landing. An instant later he was on his feet and sprinting through the moonlight in the direction of the administration building. He intended to find out what was in the gray areas he had glimpsed on the wall map, and he reasoned that the logical place to begin his investigation was with any files Jonathan Pilgrim might keep in his office.

He waited in the darkness outside the administration building as a security guard rolled by in a golf cart, then hurried to the main entrance. He had brought with him the simple tools he would need to pick the lock and short-circuit the alarm system he had glimpsed earlier; however, when he glanced through the glass doors at the entrance, he could see that the red warning light on the central control box was dark. The alarm system was off.

The doors opened when Veil pushed on them. He entered the building, pressed up against a wall in the small lobby, and listened. He heard nothing. Skirting pools of moonlight, he moved across the lobby and climbed a flight of stairs to the reception area where he had been interrogated. The door to Jonathan Pilgrim's office was open. Veil stepped into the director's office. He was searching for a light switch on the wall when a wooden match popped and flared in the darkness fifteen feet away.

He dropped to one knee, snatched the .38 from his waistband, and used both hands to steady and aim it at the spot where he had seen the flame. A moment later the air was filled with the redolent aroma of cigar smoke.

"It's about time you got here, Kendry." Jonathan Pilgrim's voice was dry, laconic. "I was getting bored. You'll find the light switch just to the left of the door."

Veil remained silent and crouched.

"Hit the lights, Kendry," Pilgrim continued after a pause, a slight edge of impatience to his tone. "They can't be seen from outside. Believe me, there's nobody here but us chickens. If you were going to be messed with, it would have happened long before you got this far. Important people do come here on occasion, and I do know something about putting together a security net. How about giving me a little credit for not being a dummy, huh?"

Veil reached back over his head with his left hand and turned on the lights. Pilgrim was seated across the room with his feet propped up on his desk. Next to his hand were an open can of Budweiser and a heavy glass ashtray with three cigar butts in it. The map Veil had seen earlier was still drawn down. There was no one else in the room.

Veil slowly straightened up. As when they had first met, he experienced a sudden, eerily powerful feeling of kinship with the astronaut; it seemed the height of silliness for him to be aiming a gun at the man. "You seem to have been expecting me," Veil said tightly as he clicked on the safety and slipped the gun back into the waistband of his jeans.

Pilgrim shrugged. "I figured you'd be back, even without the invitation I extended when I let you see this map. I take it that you weren't too impressed with our show?"

"Who is Parker?"

"He really is a lieutenant—a lieutenant colonel. He's with the Defense Intelligence Agency. He's supposed to act as a liaison between the Pentagon and the Institute."

"Supposed to?"

"Parker spends half his time dreaming up and trying to run dangerous, off-the-wall experiments, and the other half trying to keep me from finding out about them."

"Most of your budget comes from the Defense Department, doesn't it?"

"Unfortunately, a big part of it."

"Were the police even called?"

"Nope."

"How did you know I'd be able to get back in here?"

"Good instincts," Pilgrim said with a broad smile. "Let's just say I had a sneaking suspicion that you're a bit more than a very talented artist who augments his income by working as a kind of 'street detective,' helping a lot of people nobody else would pay any attention to. Incidentally, I like the way you accept bartered goods and services in exchange for your help. Nice touch. You seem to get involved in more than your share of heavy cases, and now and then you'll make the papers. You have a lot of admirers in the NYPD, but a lot of other cops and city officials wish to hell you had an investigator's license just so they could pull it. I don't know about your friends, but you've made all the right enemies."

"You know a lot about me," Veil said carefully. "I don't recall providing any of that information during my intake interview."

"On the contrary, I don't think we know much about you at all—at least not some very important things. Henry's a damn good investigator, and we always do heavy research on prospective guests before we issue an invitation to come here. With you, we ran into some problems."

"What kinds of problems?" Veil asked, his voice flat.

"1963 to 1972."

"I was in the Army."

"Indeed. Henry has access to service records. Yours covers about three-quarters of a page. It says something about a six-month hitch in Saigon as a driver in a motor pool, and the rest of the time spent as trainer and adviser to various National Guard units. What do you make of that?"

"I don't make anything of it. It's my service record. I didn't have a very distinguished career."

"I think it's bullshit. They gave you a medical discharge, labeled you a psycho. Now, I can understand how working with some of those National Guard units could drive a man crazy—but I don't believe it happened to you."

"Believe it, Jonathan."

"Henry checked, and he couldn't find a single person in any of those units who'd ever heard of you. Some very heavy people have tried to erase nine years of your life. Not only were they sloppy, but they had to be in a real big hurry. It was a patchwork job; when it seemed to be working, nobody bothered to go back and do it right. Everybody involved just breathed a great collective sigh of relief and went on about their other business."

"You could have saved me a hell of a lot of trouble if you'd just told me yesterday that I could stick around."

"Why change the subject?"

"Because it's a pointless discussion. There's no mystery there, just botched records. Why didn't you talk to me yesterday? Don't you trust Ibber?"

"Oh, I trust Henry. Let's just say that I wanted to see how committed you were. Some men simply would have gone home."

"What do you want from me, Jonathan?"

"That was some number you did on the guy who came after you."

"Maybe it happened the way I said it did."

"Being with NASA, I never made it to 'Nam," Pilgrim said as he puffed thoughtfully on his cigar and stared hard at Veil. "Still, we got our fair share of feedback. One of the stories we heard was about a guy with a move like yours, a martial arts master who could tear out a man's esophagus with his fingers. He'd won a bucketful of medals in South Vietnam, and then he was sent into Laos to help the Hmong tribes there fight the Pathet Lao. He was supposed to be a kind of one-man army, a very serious bad-ass. To tell you the truth, I never believed all the stories until I saw what was left of Golden Boy in the locker room and realized that you were the man they'd been talking about."

"Don't ever repeat any of that, Jonathan," Veil said softly. "It's for your own good."

"There's more to the story, although details are very fuzzy. Rumor had it that the brass and politicians were drumming up a big PR campaign to publicize this guy's war exploits, to win back the hearts and minds of Americans for the war effort. Then something very nasty happened in those jungles, and no one ever talked about this guy again. It seems he'd done something to make everyone's shit list. I've always wondered—"

"Jonathan, you're not listening," Veil interrupted. He slowly raised his right hand and pointed the index finger like a gun at Pilgrim's forehead. "If I were this man, I'd warn you about the danger of idly speculating about secrets nobody wants known. Repeat what you've just said to me to the wrong people and somebody could very well come to kill you. Do you understand?"

Pilgrim continued to stare at Veil for some time, then slowly nodded. "I hear you," he said evenly. "You must have fucked somebody over good."

"Who was the man in the locker room?"

"You want a beer?"

"Sure."

Pilgrim reached down to the floor, removed a sweaty can of Budweiser from an ice bucket, and tossed it across the room to Veil. He pulled the tab on the can, then went and sat down on the edge of Pilgrim's desk.

"I promise you we'll get to Golden Boy," Pilgrim said, "but first I'd like to ask you something. Your background notwithstanding, that guy should have had your ass. You're pushing forty; Golden Boy was young, trained constantly, and it was a situation he'd prepared for carefully. These things I know, Veil, so we can dispense with the mugger story. By rights, he should have been able to kill you before you even knew he was in the neighborhood. In exchange for information about Golden Boy, I'd like to know how you managed to take him."

"Why?"

"Just curious. Where did he slip up?"

"He didn't."

"Oh?"

"He came after me in the pool, not the locker room. I was warned."

"How?"

Veil sighed. "Jonathan, you won't believe me."

"Try me. I've been known to believe six impossible things before breakfast."

"Do you believe in a 'sixth sense'?"

"I certainly do. As a matter of fact, we've done a good deal of research here on what some people call 'sixth sense.'"

"I seem to have been born with a kind of sonic 'sixth sense.' When I'm in danger, I hear a sound inside my head."

"What kind of a sound?"

"It's like a chime . . . a velvet-covered chime struck by a velvet-covered hammer. It begins very softly, as something I can actually feel, as well as hear, behind my eyes. It will grow increasingly louder as the danger increases. It's saved my life a good many times. It saved my life in the pool, since it gave me time to turn around and see the man coming. After that, I really did just get lucky."

"Interesting," Pilgrim said, and took a sip of beer.

Veil felt curiously disarmed by Pilgrim's reaction, or lack of it. "You believe me?"

Now Pilgrim seemed genuinely surprised. "Why shouldn't I believe you?"

"You're the first person I've ever told about the chime. There are times when I'm not sure I believe it myself. But it does happen."

Pilgrim shrugged. "Oh, I'm sure it does. I can assure you that I've investigated some very strange things that turned out to be true. That's what the Institute is all about. Perhaps one day we'll look into this chime thing."

"Your turn, Jonathan. Tell me about Golden Boy."

"Right," Pilgrim said, perfunctorily mashing out his cigar in the ashtray. His voice had taken on an edge. "I don't know *who* he was, but I know *what* he was. After what happened, that son of a bitch Parker was forced to tell Henry and me a few things. Golden Boy belonged to the Army. He was a member of an experimental, ultra-elite unit the Army's doing some funny things with."

Pilgrim reached behind his head and tapped the map with his hook, indicating the unlabeled gray area in the valley between the two mountains. "He came out of here," the director continued, "and there are at least a half dozen more in there like him. They're code-named Mambas, and they're assassins—probably among the best in the world. Our answer to terrorism; people sic assassins on us or our friends, we sic ours on them. They're trained in ninjitsu techniques by a couple of Japanese masters, and Parker crapped brass bars when he learned that a Greenwich Village artist who paints funny pictures took one of them out. He damn well knows that you're not the average artsy type, but he doesn't know what to do about it. Are you a CIA operative, Veil? Did they fool with your records because they had better things in mind for you than sending you out on lecture tours?"

"Don't you share your information—and guesses—with Parker?"

"No. Let him use his own investigators. If he's made any connection between you and that other business I mentioned, he didn't say anything to Henry or me. *He* certainly didn't send Golden Boy after you, which makes him one very confused and worried man."

Veil thought about it, decided that Pilgrim was probably right. If Parker had somehow been involved in the assassination attempt, for whatever reason, he certainly would not have told the director and the Institute's investigator about the Mambas. "So," he said at last, "the Institute trains assassins."

Pilgrim flushed slightly. "We don't train them, the Army does."

"The land in the valley belongs to the Army?"

"They lease it from the Institute."

"If you don't like what they're doing, why don't you throw them out?"

"It's not quite that simple. Keeping the Institute functioning properly requires me to whore a little. Without Pentagon money, this place wouldn't be half of what it is. A lot of valuable work wouldn't get done. It's a trade-off—except that Parker and a few other officers over there are constantly stepping over the lines drawn in our contract. The original deal was that I'd allow the Pentagon to set up a compound on leased land, and they would have the right to monitor the experiments we conducted. Well, Parker is in the habit of using raw data he gets from here to set up his own experiments, and he thinks I'm a pain in the ass for demanding to know things he considers none of my business. Well, it's *my* operation—although some people over there would dearly love to force me out."

"Can they do that?"

"Not legally. That doesn't keep them from constantly pressuring me to step aside, or allow them greater latitude to use our facilities and staff as they see fit. There's been quite a power struggle going on here for the past few years."

"Why is the Institute so important to them?"

"We're in the business of finding out more about human beings; we're the cutting edge of that research, acknowledged by virtually everyone to be the best overall facility in the world. Armies—all armies—are in the business of controlling people. Information is power, of course, and so they see all our work as being of potentially great military significance. They couldn't duplicate our research because—as a straight military operation—they wouldn't be able to attract the subjects or research scientists we do. The Pentagon would very much like me simply to act as a front for them, and I won't do that. For now, at least, the integrity of the Institute is only as solid as my personal integrity."

"You still haven't explained what it is you want from me, Jonathan."

"*Are* you CIA?"

"I was," Veil said after a long pause. Pilgrim had been very candid, and Veil knew that he would have to begin to respond in kind if he were to get the information he had come for. His life probably depended on it. "It was a long time ago—in another lifetime. Now you could say that our relations are a bit strained."

"Strained enough for them to want to kill you?"

Veil didn't answer.

Pilgrim nodded and waved his hand in a gesture of dismissal, as if the answer were now self-evident. "It's no big surprise that you're agency-trained, you know. Not after what you did."

"Why not KGB?"

"Ah. That possibility is what worries Parker. Rest assured that there are Defense Intelligence people waiting to pick you up at La Guardia. They want to take you someplace of their own choosing where they can *really* question you."

"It makes sense."

"I never said that Parker isn't logical."

"You don't worry that I might be an enemy agent?"

"No."

"Why not?"

"Good vibes bother you?"

"The possibility that you've managed to drug me bothers me. From the first, I've felt as if I've known you all my life. There are people I've known for years, and I can't think of *any* circumstances under which I'd admit to them that I'd once worked for the CIA. I told you and it was easy. There's a strange chemistry between us, Pilgrim, and I'm not sure if I like it. It makes me uneasy."

Pilgrim laughed as he put a match to another cigar. "I think you're showing a little residual paranoia. Under the circumstances, that's not hard to understand. I can't say why you feel free to talk to me, but I can give you my reasons for trusting you. For openers, you're an artist; you spend too much time by yourself, or with the wrong people, to be an effective intelligence agent. When you're not painting, you're helping an odd assortment of people less sensitive souls might consider real losers. I mean, how many state secrets can you extract from bag ladies, Bowery bums, jugglers, and street musicians? Finally, the only reason you're here at the Institute is because I invited you. That's the end of my case."

"Except that you still haven't told me what you expect to happen now."

"What I want from you is the reason that man tried to kill you. Do you think the CIA used him to try to settle this mysterious old score you won't tell me about?"

"It's possible."

"How possible?"

Veil shrugged. "I can't quote odds. Keeping me hanging is part of the punishment; I can be executed at any time, in any place. But, when they do take me out, they won't want to leave a trace; I'll just disappear. They've already waited years, so it wouldn't make much sense for them to move on me here, in a swimming pool. There's another possibility, and you're not going to like it."

"Try me."

"Whoever recognized me, or knew I was coming here, thought, like you, that I might still be working for the agency. They assumed that my job was to put *them* out of business, so they decided to move on me first."

Pilgrim grunted with annoyance. "It means the Institute has some unwelcome guests."

"Right. I can't be certain, but I don't think the guests are CIA. Golden Boy was a double agent, but he was still just running an errand for his controller. That man or woman is still here, and I have to find out who it is; it could make a difference in my future plans."

"Shit," Pilgrim said. He sipped at his beer, grimaced. "It's not bad enough that the Pentagon is trying to screw me; now I've got foreigners lining up on my ass too. Did you recognize anyone at the reception?"

"Only the obvious celebrities. But there were a lot of people there, and I wasn't looking for anyone. If there's someone here I'd recognize as an enemy, that person is constantly on guard and watching."

Pilgrim stared at the ceiling for a few seconds, then abruptly reached down into the ice bucket and withdrew two more cans of beer. He pushed one across the desk to Veil, who left it unopened. "It would seem that our interests converge," Pilgrim said thoughtfully. "We both want to find out who controlled the assassin, and I need to find out what he wants here."

"Isn't that obvious? He's spying on the military."

"Not so obvious. The Army runs a totally separate operation, and their compound is sealed off. Henry and I are the only people who can go in there, and Parker is the only military official who's allowed to come here. You were to be my guest, not theirs. Did you tell anyone you were coming here?"

"Only the owner of the gallery that shows my work. He's not a suspect, and he wouldn't tell anyone else."

"Then you could have been made by someone who saw you at the reception."

"Dr. Ibber did a heavy research job on me. That certainly could have set off warning tremors, and somebody could have figured that the research was just a cover to establish a reason for my being invited to the Institute."

"That's possible. But it still doesn't tell me why any intelligence agency, American or foreign, would bother to spy on *my* operation. If anyone wants to know what we're doing here, all he has to do is subscribe to our journals and newsletter. We're always looking for new subscribers."

"Parker obviously thinks that your work is important—and sensitive."

"Sure. But it's not classified. I won't allow any of our research to be classified. What people *do* with the data is another matter, as long as they don't expect to use our facilities or research staff, but the data *is* published."

"Maybe somebody wants to make certain of that."

"It wouldn't take long to verify, and it wouldn't require a spy network."

"Are you going to tell Parker that he's been infiltrated?"

"No. Not yet, at any rate."

Veil raised his eyebrows slightly. "Why not?"

"Because I want answers to my own questions first, before Parker has a chance to screw things up and send our spies running for cover. Also, to be perfectly frank, I'd like to be in a position to use any information I get to counter future pressures from Parker and the Pentagon. If Parker gets loose on this thing, he'll cut me out." Pilgrim paused and puffed on his cigar. "That's it, Veil. Can we work on this problem together?"

"That suits me fine. The problem is that I'm working blind, and the person I'm after knows me. Golden Boy's controller knows I'll be coming for him. He'll be taking extra precautions, and he has all the advantages."

Pilgrim took his feet off his desk and stood up. "Then we'll have to do what we can to even the odds. You'll need some kind of disguise, and a secure base to work from."

Veil pointed to the map on the wall. "The second gray area?"

"Right."

"What's there?"

"You'll see." Pilgrim picked up the telephone on his desk and punched out a three-digit number. Veil heard a faint click on the other end, then a woman's voice blurred by fatigue.

"Yes, Jonathan?"

"Sorry about the missed sleep, Sharon. Our friend finally showed up. We're coming over."

Chapter 7

The cable car moved smoothly across the chasm between the two mountain peaks. In the valley a thousand feet below them, dawn seeped like a blood tide across the tops of trees and glinted like rubies on the surface of a clear, swift-running river. To the east, the ominous wall and electrified fence sealing off the army compound ran like an ugly scar across the face of the verdant valley.

"Parker's over there right now wondering where the hell you are and stewing in his own juices because you didn't show up in New York," Pilgrim said wryly.

"Can you get me in there?"

"Tough. Like I told you, Henry and I are the only outsiders who have free access. Even if I could manage to get you in, what would you do over there? You can't exactly stroll around a top-secret military complex."

Veil smiled thinly. "I'm very sneaky."

"I don't doubt it for a moment. But you really wouldn't want Parker to catch you inside his compound, Veil. The way things stand, you don't want him and his people to catch you alone anywhere—and certainly not at the center of his own damn spiderweb. I'm not sure I could help you."

"The man sent to kill me came out of there," Veil replied evenly. "If I can't find who and what I'm looking for in your complex, then I have to try to take a look at Parker's operation and personnel."

"I'll give some thought to the problem."

Veil stepped to the front of the car and looked out. Clouds of mist were rising off the face of the second mountain, and he could see what appeared to be a cluster of wooden buildings set in a clearing. Higher up on the mountain was a white structure that looked like a hospital. Trails branched in all directions from the central compound, and many led to large wooden chalets scattered among the trees. The atmosphere seemed elegiac, pastoral.

The cable car was fast approaching the lip of a steel-and-concrete landing platform cut into the side of the mountain. Extending out from the platform was an observation deck. A puff of wind momentarily swept away a cloud of mist, and Veil was astonished to see the unmistakable figure of a man who was generally acknowledged to be the greatest living painter and sculptor, an artist whose raw talent and breadth of vision were constantly being compared to Picasso's. Despite the early-morning chill, the man was standing at the railing of the observation deck clad only in shorts, T-shirt, and sneakers. His huge, coal-black eyes stared out over the valley in the direction of the rising sun. Veil stepped back to avoid being seen, and Pilgrim casually saluted with his hook as they passed over the spot where the man was standing.

"That was Perry Tompkins," Veil said, making no effort to mask his surprise.

"Yeah."

"Tompkins supposedly disappeared over six months ago; it made headlines all over the world. People in a dozen different countries are still searching for him."

44

"Obviously, Perry didn't disappear. He simply came here. Those he chose to confide in know where he is, and Perry's friends aren't in the habit of talking to the press."

"What is this place, and what's Tompkins doing here?"

Pilgrim reached around Veil and pushed a red button on the emergency control panel next to the sliding door. The car immediately stopped, gently swayed for a few seconds, then was still. "This is the Institute's hospice," the director said evenly. "Sharon—Dr. Solow—who was supposed to give you a battery of psychological tests before somebody got the notion to kill you, heads it. It's also where she conducts what she describes as near-death studies, a long-range project examining the changes in attitude, perception, and consciousness some people undergo as they are dying. Perry is dying, and he accepted our invitation to come here and share the experience of this last transition with Sharon. Most of the hospice guests, like Perry, are in the last stages of terminal illness, but there are also a few men and women we call Lazarus People who come here to be studied."

"People come here to let you watch them die?"

"Watch and study, yes. They're people who are approaching their own deaths with a certain measure of equanimity and a great deal of curiosity. Do you find that unsettling?"

"It takes some getting used to."

"Of course. That's one reason why we don't publicize the hospice facility. Another is the fact that, from time to time, we have some very famous people here, and we want to insure maximum security and privacy. The hospice is the most private place at the Institute. This cable car provides the only access to it, and the car is key-operated. Only residents and staff of the hospice are allowed to use it."

"What are 'Lazarus People'?"

"Do you know the difference between clinical and biological death?"

"The way I understand it, clinical death is when heartbeat and respiration stop; the person can still be revived, if action is taken quickly enough. Biological death involves the deterioration of the brain and other organs, and it's for keeps."

Pilgrim nodded. "That's it. A small percentage of men and women who've survived clinical death—on the operating table, from electric shock, drowning, or whatever—report an out-of-body experience and the glimpsing of a bright portal of light that we call the Lazarus Gate. Along with certain other characteristics, these experiences define Lazarus People. What's so fascinating is the fact that the phenomenon Lazarus People describe is remarkably consistent, whether the person comes from Kansas or the Kalahari. It seems to be universal, culture-free."

"What about you? Did you see this Lazarus Gate when your plane crashed?"

Pilgrim smiled thinly. "I suffered clinical death the good, old-fashioned way—I don't remember a thing. It's not an experience I look forward to repeating, although—interestingly enough—Lazarus People usually do."

"Privacy is one thing, secrecy something else. I can't remember ever reading anything about near-death studies in connection with the Institute."

"This isn't an area of research we put a lot of emphasis on, and we don't publish our findings."

"Why not?"

"The Institute is a hard-science operation. That's our image, and our meal ticket. Near-death studies have the sort of mystical, hocus-pocus aura about it that gets you featured in the kinds of newspapers they sell at supermarket checkout stands. We don't need that."

Veil thought about it, nodded in agreement. "What are the other characteristics of these 'Lazarus People'?"

"Some other time, Veil, if you don't mind," Pilgrim said, glancing at his watch. He pushed a green button on the control box, and the car started moving again. "Sharon's been up all night, and we're all tired."

"How do the people you want to study find out about this place?"

"We have a network of people around the world who serve the hospice, as well as the rest of the Institute; they keep us informed of people who might warrant, and welcome, an

46

invitation. Also, certain people—artists like Perry Tompkins, for example—are told of the hospice's existence and its purpose. If the situation arises, and if they so desire, they have an open invitation to join us. In return, they agree to share their last experience with us, as best they can."

"And all of this to study *death*?"

"To study the *passage* from life to death. We know that Lazarus People experience a sudden shift in consciousness as a result of unexpected, and sometimes violent, death, but there's some evidence to indicate that certain people with terminal illness also go through unique shifts in consciousness as they approach death. Sharon is trying to chart and codify those shifts."

"How does she do that?"

"Mostly through a succession of in-depth interviews and specialized tests she has developed. I'm sure she'll be happy to explain the details, if you're interested."

"Who'll know I'm over here?"

"Just Sharon and myself."

"Not Dr. Ibber?"

Pilgrim shook his head.

"You said you trusted Ibber."

"Trust isn't the point. If I were to tell everyone I trusted, then most of the staff at the Institute would know. Henry has nothing to do with the hospice; he doesn't even have access. I figured it would be best to keep the fact of your presence here on a strict need-to-know basis."

"Good. Am I supposed to be terminally ill, or a Lazarus Person?"

"Neither. You'll find that the day-in, day-out close proximity to death makes people hypersensitive and aware. Each guest jealously guards his and everyone else's privacy, and it's almost impossible to fool or lie to these people for very long. It wouldn't take long for somebody to spot you as a ringer. You'll be staff, on some kind of special assignment; Sharon screens and hires her people personally, usually on recommendations from her colleagues. As soon as we rig some disguise for you to wear, you'll be free to come and go as you please. In the meantime, I'll try to figure out some way to get you into the military compound—if you're sure you want to go."

"I'm sure. When will I meet Dr. Solow?"

"Now," the director said as the car bumped gently into its berth in the side of the mountain. Pilgrim slid open the door and motioned for Veil to exit first.

He stepped out onto the platform. The woman standing to his right was an inch or two over five feet, with long, silky blond hair that fell straight across her back. Her eyes were a pale, glacial blue and, in the light of dawn, appeared to be streaked with silver. Obviously cold, she was huddled in a worn green suede jacket that was too large for her. She wore sneakers and faded jeans that emphasized her slim legs and hips. Even with fatigue etched deeply into her face, Veil considered her the most beautiful woman he had ever seen. She was, he thought, about his own age, and he found himself looking down at her left hand; she wore no wedding band.

"Hello, Mr. Kendry," the woman said brightly, stepping forward and extending her hand. "I'm Sharon Solow."

"Pleased to meet you, Dr. Solow," Veil replied softly, staring into the silver-streaked blue eyes and holding the soft, tapered hand a second longer than necessary.

"Hello, Captain Hook," Sharon Solow said as Pilgrim stepped up to her and kissed her forehead. "How have you been?"

"A bit distracted," the astronaut answered with a wry smile and a quick glance in Veil's direction. "How have you been?"

"For the past few hours, extremely curious."

The greeting was rather formal, Veil thought, but the exchange had a bittersweet quality that, for some reason, made him feel terribly sad. Embarrassed and shaken by the power of his physical and emotional reaction to Sharon Solow, Veil quickly looked away; in the space of a few seconds, the sight of this woman and the touch of her hand had made him feel depths of pain, longing, and loneliness he had not known he had. He now realized how many sights, sounds, smells, and feelings had rushed past him during the course of his life;

they were things he had never given a second thought to until this moment.

When Veil looked back, he was surprised to find Sharon Solow studying him.

"Well?" the woman continued, raising her eyebrows slightly and tilting her head toward Pilgrim. "Is he, or isn't he?"

"Once upon a time," Pilgrim answered. "He's a real heavyweight, but he promotes his own fights now."

"I think I'm missing something," Veil said, looking at Pilgrim.

"Jonathan told me he thought you worked for the CIA," Sharon Solow said, still studying Veil intently. "He also ventured the opinion that you were a good guy, and Jonathan is very good at telling the good guys from the bad."

Veil shrugged. "I'm flattered."

"Sharon," Pilgrim said, "I don't want anyone to see Veil until I can rig some kind of disguise; he needs to be able to wander around the main complex incognito. Do you have a place where he can hole up?"

"Good grief," the woman said in a joking tone that was laced with nervousness and tension. "Am I entitled to an explanation?"

"You certainly are, m'dear, and you will get it in living color and full stereo. But not now, if you don't mind. I'm beat." Pilgrim paused, glanced sharply at Veil. "I think we're all beat, and explanations can wait a few hours. It will probably be late afternoon before I get back."

"Jonathan, I must ask you something. Will Veil's presence here pose a danger to any of my people?"

"No. Our problem is on the other mountain."

"Then why does he have to wear a disguise here?"

"I don't want to risk being described to some outsider over the telephone," Veil answered. "Also, it's simply wise to take every precaution."

"Precaution against *what*?" the woman persisted.

"Later, Sharon," the director said quietly. "I appreciate your concern for your people, but I'll have to ask you to trust me."

Sharon Solow sighed, nodded. "Of course I trust you, Jonathan. For the time being, Veil can stay in the storeroom adjacent to my office. It has a cot. When he's disguised to your satisfaction, I can either put him up in a chalet or an apartment in staff quarters."

"Make it a chalet—and a remote one. If anyone asks, say he's a new staff member who needs the peace and quiet of a chalet for the special work he's doing. I want Veil to have maximum privacy so he can come and go without attracting undue attention."

"I'll take care of it, Jonathan."

Pilgrim lit a cigar. "I'll see the two of you later."

The woman smiled wanly. "Get some sleep, Captain Hook. We both know how much you need it."

Pilgrim stepped back into the cable car and closed the door after him. A moment later the car lifted from the platform and began its return journey to the top of the mountain on the other side of the valley.

Sharon Solow watched the car for almost a minute before she finally turned and smiled at Veil. "This way to the Solow Hilton, Mr. Kendry," she said, pointing to her right to indicate a path cut into the side of the mountain.

Chapter 8

Veil dreams.

Dawn will break in two hours; Veil's plane will leave at three. Through the night Veil has walked the streets of Saigon, fording garish rainbow rivers of neon, flinching at the sound of disembodied groans, screams, sighs, grunts, and whispered invitations that reverberate in his ears like gunshots.

Veil does not rest like other men, whom sleep renews through dream-discharge of terror, rage, frustration, and forbidden desire; dreams do not flash across the surface of his consciousness to cleanse his mind. Like now, Veil hangs suspended in dreams like a diver in a clear sea roiled by things that sometimes soothe, but more often rend. He is still more than a year away from learning how to control, to roll away from, his night journeys, and physical exhaustion is the only thing he has found that will sink him to the bottom of the sea and give him peace; violence is his most potent narcotic.

It has been this way all his life, and there has never been anyone to understand. The fever that burned his brain made him irrevocably different from other children, as it now sets him apart from other men. Bright, a fast learner who excelled at athletics, Veil was also tormented and hyperactive; filled with rage and terror, he was unpredictable, often uncontrollable, dangerous. Peers and adults feared him, for good reason. It was inevitable that he would come to the attention of the police and the courts.

The Army, to which he escaped and which accepted him at seventeen, was his salvation. In the service of his country, Veil found redemption—for, with the acquisition of discipline, precisely those qualities of fierceness and physical strength that made him a threat to others outside the armed forces, became a valuable asset to those in command inside. He was first in his basic training group, first in advanced armored training, first in Officer Candidate School, first in his training group with Special Forces, where he was recruited by the Central Intelligence Agency. Within six months he was fighting in Vietnam, where he discovered that combat left in its wake welcome, renewing oblivion.

With the meeting in the jungle clearing, all this has changed. His period of indoctrination in Tokyo has left him increasingly disturbed at night, and no amount of exercise seems to help. He is fearful of the future, does not know if he can carry out his new assignment, does not know if he can remain sane without war.

"Hey, soldier. Want girl? Clean girl. Virgin. Twenty dollar."

The pimp's voice has come out of the shadows of a doorway. Veil keeps walking, stiffens as someone grabs his arm.

"How about boy, soldier? Clean boy. Also twenty dollar."

Veil looks down at the cowering, trembling children the Vietnamese has dragged in front of him. He feels short of breath, as if he is plunging into a vacuum, hears an agonized groan that he realizes comes from his own throat. Veil knows this boy and girl, knows their names, has played with them and told them stories about America. They are Hmong children, members of the tribe he left six weeks before.

"What you say, soldier? You be sport. You take both. Thirty dollar for thirty minutes."

Veil stabs at the eyes of the Vietnamese, then rolls away from the dream.

Chapter 9

Veil awoke with a start, momentarily disoriented by the intensity of his dream-memory. Then he remembered where he was. He took a number of deep breaths, then sat up on the swaybacked Army cot and looked at his watch. It was four-thirty. The warm, late-afternoon sunlight that lanced through the leaves of the surrounding trees filled the room with strange, shifting, chiaroscuro patterns of light and dark; branches swayed in a gentle breeze and scraped against the sides of the wooden building with a pleasant sound like wire brushes on a snare drum.

The nutty smell of rich, fresh-brewed coffee that permeated the air came from a Silex pot set on a hot plate across the room. Next to the hot plate was an array of toilet articles in their original packaging. Veil rose and poured himself a cup of coffee, carrying it and the toilet articles into a small bathroom

55

where he shaved and washed himself. He refilled his cup, then opened the door and stepped into the adjoining office.

Sharon Solow was seated at the keyboard of a large computer console at the opposite end of the spacious office. To her left was a sheaf of papers to which she would occasionally refer as she tapped on the keys. Tiers of symbols that Veil did not understand flashed sporadically across the console's display screen. Sharon was dressed now in a white lab coat worn over a plaid skirt, flesh-colored stockings, and low-heeled black pumps. Her hair was tied back in a ponytail that arced gracefully away from her neck and cascaded down almost to the small of her back. There was a faint aroma of expensive perfume, and Veil felt a curious sense of intimacy at the sight of the woman working, unaware of his presence.

The walls and ceiling of the office were painted a flat white, and the only decoration was an enlarged black-and-white photograph mounted on the wall above and behind the console. It was an eerie and beautiful photo, captured by a camera that had been positioned half in and half out of a vast body of water. The surface of the sea was absolutely still and flat all the way to the horizon. Beneath the surface, just barely visible in the murky depths, a fish had been caught in the middle of a half turn; in the distance, not much larger than a speck even in the blowup, a lone gull soared high in the cloudless sky as it rode thermal drafts. There were two levels of existence, two different creatures inhabiting the same world, but separated from each other by a membrane at the cusp of air and water that was at once dimensionless and as impenetrable as eternity.

Finally sensing Veil's presence, the woman turned in her chair, nodded, and smiled warmly. "Hi," she said easily.

Veil felt a tug in his chest as he gazed into the blue eyes that still, even in entirely different light, appeared to be streaked with silver. "Hi. Thanks for the coffee. It's excellent. I like the Solow Hilton."

"I'm glad. I thought you might like some coffee when you woke up. I brought the pot in about a half hour ago. Did I wake you?"

"No. Would you like a cup?"

Sharon shook her head. "You must be starving. If you'd like, I'll have the commissary send something over. If you can hold out, I've ordered dinner to be delivered at seven. Jonathan should be here by then."

"I'll hold out, but I'd expected to talk to Jonathan before then. Do you know where I can reach him?"

"He'll be sleeping, Mr. Kendry." Sharon said with just the slightest trace of a frown. "Besides the obvious injuries, the plane crash damaged Jonathan's adrenal system. He won't slow down, and he won't take medication, but he's very prone to exhaustion. Being up all night will have taken its toll. He forces himself to get by on six or seven hours of sleep, but most men with his condition would sleep eleven or twelve out of every twenty-four."

"Pilgrim's quite a man."

The woman raised her eyebrows slightly. "He certainly is. I have a strong suspicion that he feels the same way about you."

"Did he tell you anything about my situation?"

Sharon's hair rippled like wheat-colored water as she again shook her head. "I've seen Dr. Ibber's file on you, of course, and I've read the transcript of your intake interview; I was supposed to carry out some preliminary psychological testing on you. But I expect that what I've seen is just the tip of the iceberg. Jonathan called me yesterday morning soon after you'd left. At least Jonathan thought you'd left. He said there'd been some trouble." She paused, smiled wryly. "Jonathan just casually mentioned in passing that he was sure you were a CIA agent, thought there was a good chance you'd sneak back, and he wanted a place for you to hide where only the three of us would know where you were."

"He didn't say anything else?"

"He told me I didn't want to know the rest, which meant that *he* didn't want me to know the rest."

"And you didn't ask?"

"No."

"You seem to have an excellent working relationship," Veil said carefully.

"Yes, I'd say we do."

"Would it be presumptuous of me to ask if your relationship extends beyond that?"

"Yes, it would."

"Then I apologize, Doctor."

Sharon smiled, winked mischievously. "But I'll answer, anyway. Jonathan and I are just good friends." Suddenly the smile slipped from the woman's face; her eyes went slightly out of focus, and her tone became distant. "Jonathan's in love with a woman no other woman on earth can compete with."

"She must be some lady."

"Oh, that she is," Sharon said in the same curiously distant, flat tone. "She's Death."

Veil's first reaction was that the woman was making some kind of macabre joke—but if she was, her face gave no indication of it. Veil waited for her to say something else, but Sharon seemed lost in thought. The silence in the office grew awkward.

"Excuse me," he said at last, starting to retreat back into the storeroom. "You have work to do, and I've interrupted."

"Oh, no. Stay if you'd like, Mr. Kendry." The bright sheen in Sharon Solow's voice had returned as quickly as it had vanished, and her eyes were once again in focus. "You're probably curious about what I'm up to over on this mountain."

Veil leaned against the doorjamb, folded his arms across his chest and grinned. "More than a bit, Doctor."

"All right, let's start with the technology; aside from our hospital equipment, this computer is just about all the technology there is—and I don't really need this. Our work here just doesn't lend itself to machinery."

"It's subjective."

"Almost totally." Sharon nodded toward the papers, then the display screen. "Right now I'm collating the weekly anecdotal reports from some of our residents, whom I'm sure

Jonathan has told you are in various stages of terminal illness."

"Yes. Jonathan gave me some idea of what you're trying to do. If you'll pardon me for saying so, I'm not sure I see the point. It seems to me that you're like a film editor who works on nothing but final sequences."

"Indeed," Sharon replied in a firm voice, "but many films have been saved by the final sequence; those last frames can bring everything together and illuminate all that has gone before."

Veil thought about it, nodded. "All right."

"Then, of course, there's always the possibility that what we call death may not be an end at all—only a transition."

"And Lazarus People may have already made that transition and come back to tell about it?"

Sharon seemed vaguely surprised. "Jonathan obviously trusts you a great deal to talk about Lazarus People so soon."

"Why?"

"It's a sensitive subject because it has so many obvious religious overtones. We don't approach it from that angle at all, but Jonathan is always afraid that outsiders will think that the Institute is running some kind of elaborate ashram over here."

"I suppose he figured you'd eventually tell me about them, anyway. In any case, it seems to me that their reported out-of-body experiences could be nothing more than elaborate hallucinations triggered by trauma and shock."

"You're right, of course. But if they are hallucinations, they're remarkably consistent. Also, even though an out-of-body experience is the most dramatic characteristic of Lazarus People, there are others—all part of what we call the Lazarus Syndrome. For example, no matter how neurotic they may have been before, Lazarus People tend to emerge from their near-death experience with very integrated personalities. They begin to think in universal terms, and it's almost impossible to manipulate them with the words and symbols leaders use to manipulate so many of the rest of us. Lazarus People no longer fear death. On the contrary; even though they've become passionately life-affirming, they actually look forward to death. This duality in attitude is what we call the Lazarus Paradox."

"Impressive. Are there any other characteristics of these Lazarus People?"

"I'm not boring you?"

Veil smiled. "I'm really very interested in you and your work, Dr. Solow."

Sharon flushed slightly, but continued to meet Veil's gaze. "In that case, I'll have to tell you more about both. There seems to be generally heightened consciousness and sensitivity in all aspects of life. Lazarus People seem to recognize each other on sight, with nothing being said. It's positively uncanny."

"Mental telepathy?"

Sharon laughed and raised her eyebrows in mock distress. "Bite your tongue, Mr. Kendry. That is a term we *never* use around here. Please confine yourself to words like 'consciousness' and 'sensitivity.'"

"Agreed."

"Good," Sharon said, her tone becoming more serious. "In that case, I'll tell you about one of the eeriest characteristics of all. For want of a better term, we call it 'soul-catching.'"

"Which is?"

"Some Lazarus People—not all, by any means—seem to experience a premonition of extreme personal danger."

"I'm not sure I understand."

"Let's suppose a Lazarus Person is about to be mugged on the street, or hit from behind in a barroom brawl. Some of these people report hearing a soft bell tone, a chiming sound, inside their heads a split second before the knife is drawn or the bottle swung. The Lazarus People who've experienced it swear that 'soul-catching' has saved their lives."

Suddenly Veil felt disoriented—short of breath, as if the woman's words had been a blow to the stomach. He had heard no chiming, but he had a distinct premonition of danger; the danger was not physical, and he did not believe it stemmed from the woman, but it was there nonetheless, coming from a source in the past, present, or future which he could not identify. He quickly looked away to hide his reaction.

"Mr. Kendry?" Sharon continued after a few seconds. "Are you all right?"

He slowly exhaled, then turned back and forced himself to smile. "Why don't you call me Veil?"

Sharon stared at him for a few moments, concern in her eyes. Veil continued to smile at her, and finally Sharon smiled back. "Very well—if you'll call me Sharon."

"Jonathan doesn't take near-death studies very seriously, does he?"

Sharon's smile vanished, and her voice became flat. "Is that what he told you?"

"It's the impression he gives."

"Well, he's understandably nervous about outsiders possibly misunderstanding the purpose of work as ambiguous—'soft' is the term he would use—as near-death studies."

"Then why does he put it under Institute aegis in the first place? He's given you a whole mountain."

"I suppose that's a question you should put to Jonathan," Sharon replied in a careful, neutral tone.

"Are you a physician? Ph.D.?"

"Both."

"Doctorate in psychology?"

Sharon nodded.

"What was your specialty before you became involved with near-death studies?"

"I've always done this kind of work. I'm a thanatologist—a specialist in death and the dying." Sharon abruptly swung around in her chair and tapped a few keys on the computer console. A wavy line plotted on a grid flashed on the screen; a red arrow indicated a sharp spike three-quarters of the way along the length of the line. "This may interest you, Veil. This is where we *think* Lazarus People have been, in a manner of speaking. Did Jonathan mention the Lazarus Gate?"

"Yes. A bright portal of light."

"Well, this is what we believe the EEG of a person at the Lazarus Gate looks like. It's the pattern of brain waves a person will exhibit just before the out-of-body experience begins. This is a computer simulation, somewhat simplified."

"How did you come up with that?"

"Hospital records. A tiny percentage of people who've had near-death experiences and were later discovered to be Lazarus People were hooked up to electroencephalographs when they went into a state of clinical death. By going back over the EEG tapes, comparing them with anecdotal reports and feeding the results into a computer, we come up with this simulation of the Lazarus Gate. Of course, it's strictly a theory. A guess."

Veil felt another, stronger premonition of amorphous danger as he stared at the bright display screen. "It would be interesting to put somebody to sleep, manipulate his brain-wave patterns to match what you've got there, then see what he has to say when he wakes up."

Sharon laughed easily. "Oh, I'm sure it would be an intriguing story—and we probably could 'put' a person here with chemical and electrical stimulation. The problem is that the person wouldn't be asleep; he'd be dead. Notice the flat amplitude of the EEG pattern before and after the spike. We might be able to get a subject to the Lazarus Gate, but there's no guarantee we'd ever get him back again. It's not an experiment that's ever likely to be done."

"Has anyone ever actually passed through that 'gate' and come back?"

"Not that we know of," Sharon said hesitantly, after a long pause.

"You don't sound too certain."

"I'm certain."

"What do you think is beyond the Lazarus Gate?"

"We have no way of knowing, Veil. I suspect nothing; just death. I'm really not interested in religious matters, except in the way religious belief may effect people's attitudes and behavior as they approach death. I don't see how any kind of consciousness, call it a 'soul' or whatever, can exist independently of the electrochemical plant—the brain—which generates it. Brain tissue immediately begins to deteriorate with the onset of biological death. What we're examining is a moment in time in which consciousness—and subsequent behavior among the *living*, the *survivors*—may be radically changed. My concern is with exploring what the near-death experience can teach us about life."

Veil waited for Sharon to continue, but her pale, silver-streaked eyes now seemed to be staring inward, as if at some image in her mind that was beyond words—or beyond his comprehension. Finally she tapped a key on the console; the brain-wave pattern associated with the Lazarus Gate winked and disappeared.

"If you'll excuse me, Veil, I think I will go back to work now," Sharon continued at last, her voice very soft. "I'd like to finish collating these reports before Jonathan gets here."

"Of course. Thank you very much for the tour."

Sharon did not reply. Veil studied her back for a few moments, then stepped back into the storeroom and closed the door. He lay down on the cot, put his hands behind his head, and stared at the ceiling.

He was certain that the woman had been disturbed by some of the things he had said, or the questions he had asked, but she had tried to cover her reactions—as he had done when she'd mentioned soul-catching. Soul-catching, he thought, was a phenomenon he'd experienced all his life. Pilgrim knew of at least one instance, for Veil had told him about it in connection with the assassination attempt by the Golden Boy. Yet Pilgrim had said nothing. Veil wondered why; he wondered what, if anything, the man and woman were trying to hide.

Veil had been certain that Jonathan Pilgrim and Sharon Solow were his allies. Now he was not so sure.

Chapter 10

V eil dreams.

Madison glances up as Veil enters the small, cluttered office in the basement of the American embassy. Blood rushes to the obese man's face, and his lips curl back from his teeth in a snarl as he leaps up from his chair. "Where the fuck have you been, Kendry?!" A bloated hand with thick, stubby fingers sweeps across the top of the cheap metal desk and sends folders, a small paperweight, a framed photograph, and a half-filled cup of coffee sailing through the air to smash against the cracked plaster wall. "You were supposed to be on a fucking plane for fucking Washington twenty-seven fucking hours ago! Do you know how many generals, senators, and congressmen were standing around waiting for you with their thumbs up their asses? You left the fucking *President of the United States* standing around with his thumb—"

Too late, the CIA controller sees the murderous rage in

Veil's eyes and face, the subtle but deadly weaving of his hands, the ominous acceleration of his gait. Madison grabs for the .45 automatic in his shoulder holster. Veil shifts his weight and throws a side kick that flicks through the air with the speed of a chameleon's tongue and the force of a pile driver. The instep of his left foot snaps Madison's wrist cleanly at the joint, and the gun flies across the room to land near the coffee-stained litter already there. Madison, eyes glazing with pain and shock, clutches at his shattered right wrist and falls back into his chair.

"If you want to shout or press an alarm button, feel free," Veil says in a low voice that crackles like electricity around the edges. "Just know that the first person into this office had better be a damn good shot, and fast, because I'll snap your fat, sweaty neck the moment I hear the door open."

Madison, chest heaving as he gasps for air, manages to shake his head.

"Abort Cheshire Cat," Veil continues evenly, pointing to Madison's desk telephone. "Stop it right now."

"How did you find out?" Madison's eyes have cleared, but his voice is a fuzzy croak.

"A couple of hours before takeoff, a pimp tried to sell me a couple of kids—a boy and a girl." Now Veil's voice breaks slightly. "*Kids*, Madison. I happen to know these two; they're from my village. Your Major Po and his men have been terrorizing that tribe of Hmong, and Po's been making a little extra money on the side by selling the women and children to Saigon pimps. I killed the pimp, and I'm probably going to kill you when we're finished with our business. Then I'm going to kill Po."

"I didn't know, Kendry."

"I believe that you didn't know what Po is up to—but you knew Po, knew his reputation. I've spent the past few hours plugging into every connection we've got here, and it turns out that the good major is very well known in South Vietnam—as a black marketeer, whoremaster, and big-time dope dealer. He was getting to be too much even for the South Vietnamese, which is saying something, considering the level of corruption in Saigon. ARVN asked the Americans to find a nice quiet place to put him, and our command went to the CIA. You got the detail. When this whole idea of turning me into a toy soldier came up, you saw an opportunity to take care of two pieces of business at the same time. For chrissake, Madison, you cold-blooded son of a bitch. You turned my village over to a bloodsucker."

Madison grimaces as he uses his left hand to lift his broken wrist onto the top of the desk. Sweat pours from his face and neck, stains his shirt dark. "Come on, Kendry," he says with a grunt. "You were their adviser and trainer, not their mother."

"Shut up! I fought with those people, and at least a half dozen died for me. They hated the communists even worse than we do, and they believed the things I told them about America and Americans. In just six weeks Po was able to do something the communists hadn't been able to do in twenty years—turn that village around. It's become a Pathet Lao stronghold. Po's answer, naturally, is to mount a commando operation to kill them all off. Cheshire Cat. Pick up the phone and call it off, Madison."

"I can't, Kendry. It's an ARVN operation."

"Bullshit. We're ARVN. They'll do what you tell them."

"Not this time. They're really into Cheshire Cat, Kendry. They've been itching to cut across that border, just to prove that they can do it. The village is easy pickings, and they're hot for it."

Veil picks up Madison's .45 from the floor and sticks the muzzle into the CIA controller's ear. "Give it a bit more thought," Veil says softly. "Come up with something creative or I'm going to spray the wall with your brains. You know I'm not bluffing."

Madison continues to sweat profusely, but he does not flinch. "Killing me won't make any difference, Kendry," he says in a firm voice. "I'm telling you that I can't stop Cheshire Cat. Even if I had the juice to countermand ARVN on this thing, there isn't time. Po and his boys are on their way. Forget it. We've got more important things at stake here, and that's just gook against gook."

Veil steps back, swivels Madison around in his chair, and delivers a quick blow on the left shoulder that snaps the man's collarbone. Madison's arm flops, then goes limp in his lap. He closes his eyes and utters an animal moan of agony, but he does not cry out. "You're throwing it all away, you crazy bastard," the fat man manages to whisper.

"You threw that tribe away like yesterday's garbage."

"Listen to me, Kendry. There isn't anything I can do about Cheshire Cat, and busting me up isn't going to change that. You're going to forget that tribe, and I'm going to forget what's happened here; I just took a nasty fall. We have to think about your assignment."

Veil abruptly grabs the front of Madison's shirt, hauls the broken man out of his chair, and slams him back against the wall. Madison's snapped limbs flap, and he clenches his teeth to choke off a scream that issues from his throat as a muffled, mewing screech.

"Do exactly as I say," Veil replies evenly as he reaches for Madison's crotch and cups the man's testicles. "If you don't, I'm going to rip your balls out by the roots. I'm going to pick up this phone and dial some friends of ours. You're going to pull yourself together and issue a series of commands, and you're going to do it in your usual snide, cold, son-of-a-bitch tone. First, I want a car and driver sent to the back to take me to the airport, where there's going to be a fully armed chopper warmed up and waiting for me. I want a box of grenades, a machine pistol, and fifteen magazines loaded into the cockpit. If you won't stop Cheshire Cat, I will. And I'll kill anyone, Vietnamese or American who tries to stop me."

"Don't do this, Kendry. We're losing this war because we're losing the support of our own people. The last thing we need is a hero turned traitor. Hate me, bust me up some more if it will make you feel better, but don't do something that will cause tremendous damage to the United States of America."

"Like yesterday's garbage," Veil repeats as he picks up the receiver, dials a number, then holds the receiver to Madison's ear and mouth. "And you used me like a newspaper to wrap it in."

Veil reaches down and again cups the controller's testicles. When the orders are given, Veil rips the telephone wire from the wall. He slides the .45 into his belt, turns and heads for the door.

"Kendry!"

"Remember that anyone who tries to stop me is a dead man."

"You're the dead man, Kendry."

"I presume so," he replies evenly.

"God *damn* you! Stop and listen to me!"

Veil turns and faces Madison, who is still leaning against the wall. The fat man's sweat-soaked face is ashen with pain, but his voice is steady. His eyes glitter with rage and hate. "I won't try to stop you," Madison says, "because I don't feel like trying to explain to the world why we had to gun down our own hero in the streets of Saigon. Knowing you, you'll probably survive whatever it is you're about to do. But you're still dead meat. You were *my* man. I recommended you for this mission back in the States. You're the one turning traitor, but my ass is going to go up in smoke along with yours. I'm responsible for you. They'll try to break me for this, but I'll survive too. I want to be in a position to have you killed. One day a bullet is going to smash your brain, Kendry. It won't be right away. I may wait a few years because you're too insane to really suffer now. I think I'd like to wait and see if you ever find peace—or maybe even a little happiness. That'll be the day you die, you fucking madman. Think about that in the years to come."

Veil turns and walks out of the office, leaving the door open behind him.

Chapter 11

It was after ten P.M. by the time Veil returned to his chalet. He removed the tinted aviator glasses and black wig that comprised his simple disguise, tossed the articles on the bed, then poured himself half a tumbler full of Scotch from the well-stocked bar. It had been a long and frustrating day—long because he had been up and across the valley to the Institute's main complex before dawn; frustrating because his random search for a familiar face had been an exercise in futility. There was a good possibility that he wouldn't recognize the man he was after even if he walked past him. He had managed to cover the entire complex; he had seen many fascinating and sensitive experiments in progress, but nothing that would justify the risk and cost of setting up the kind of spy network that would include the care and feeding of an assassin like the Golden Boy. He knew that he needed a more systematic approach.

He had more faith in his dreams. His past seemed to be the key, and when he slept, his subconscious kept returning him there, allowing him to sift and sort memories in the search for a link between then and now—if there was one.

He opened a dresser drawer and took out a map of the Institute that included the hospice and the Army compound. He drained the Scotch, then set the tumbler on the gray area of the Army compound. The Golden Boy had come out of there, Veil thought, and he was going to have to find a way to get in.

"Veil?"

He turned to find Sharon Solow, her fine hair backlit by moonglow, standing in the shadows just beyond the open doorway. The muscles in his stomach and groin fluttered with surprise, pleasure, and anticipation. "Come in, Sharon," he said quietly.

The woman entered the chalet carrying a covered tray, which she set down on the rough-hewn wood table in the center of the sunken living room. She removed the gingham cloth to reveal an array of sandwiches, a bowl of tossed salad, and a carafe of red wine. "I know you missed dinner, so I thought you might like something to eat. Nothing fancy, as you can see."

"Fancy enough," Veil replied with a grin as he moved to the table. He hadn't eaten all day, and the sight and smell of the food made him realize just how hungry he was. "Thank you very much. Will you join me?"

Sharon shook her head. "I've eaten."

"Then please keep me company."

"All right," Sharon replied evenly, sitting down in the chair that Veil pulled out for her.

He sat down across from Sharon, poured two glasses of wine from the carafe, then selected a roast beef sandwich from the tray. "Delicious," he said when he had finished the first sandwich and was about to start on another. "This wasn't necessary, but it's certainly much appreciated."

"I had an ulterior motive for coming here tonight, Veil."

Veil set aside the second sandwich and looked up. Sharon was leaning forward on her elbows, chin cupped in the palms of her hands. She was staring at him intently. "Which is?"

"I'd like you to answer some questions."

"I'll try."

"What are you?"

"Just a man," Veil replied softly, sipping at his wine.

"We've established that you worked for the CIA. Are you a spy now?"

"No. Now I'm just a painter from New York City."

"I don't think I believe you," Sharon said after a long pause.

"It's true."

"What are you doing here?"

"You know what I'm doing here; I was invited."

Sharon sighed and closed her eyes for a few seconds. When she opened them, there was a glint of frustration and anger in their pale depths. "You're just using words, Veil. If you don't want me to know what's going on, simply say so. Don't play games."

"I'm sorry, Sharon. I don't mean to be rude. If you want to know what's going on, I think you should ask Jonathan."

"I'm asking you."

"You seemed content yesterday to take Jonathan's direction on this. Has something happened?"

"Let's just say that I feel a renewed sense of responsibility."

"For the hospice, or Jonathan?"

"Both."

"Where is Jonathan?"

"I don't know, Veil. Wherever he is, he went there in the helicopter just before noon. He may be in Monterey, or even San Francisco, doing research, but I can't be sure. He almost never leaves the mountain, unless it's on some kind of fund-raising business. I don't think that's what he's doing, and it makes me uneasy. That's why I'd like you to tell me what's happened."

"Somebody made a mistake, Sharon. I have to find out who made the mistake and why it was made."

"What kind of mistake?"

"A dangerous one. It involved me, but it could also affect the Institute. That's why Jonathan wants me to get to the bottom of it."

"You're not telling me anything, Veil."

"I feel in an awkward position, caught between my host and hostess. Jonathan made it very plain that he didn't want you to worry."

"Is there something to be worried about?"

"I don't know, Sharon."

The woman took a deep breath, slowly let it out. "Can what you're doing bring harm to Jonathan?"

Veil rose from the table, poured himself a second Scotch, and lit one of the few cigarettes he allowed himself each day. "I don't know the answer to that question, either," he said as he exhaled a thin stream of smoke. "I'm beginning to wonder if there isn't something he's doing, or has already done, that could harm him."

"I'm not following you."

"What are you and Jonathan hiding from me?"

The question startled the woman, causing her to stiffen in her chair. "Veil, I don't know what you mean."

He sipped at his drink, studying Sharon over the rim of the tumbler. If she was putting on an act, he thought, it was a very good one. He set the glass down, ground out his cigarette. "What else do you do over here that you haven't told me about?"

"*Nothing*." Sharon replied, a note of frustration creeping into her voice. "It's just near-death studies, and I've told you virtually everything there is to know about it. We look for changes in consciousness and behavior as people approach the cusp between life and death."

"But you also study Lazarus People, whom you believe may already have been on that cusp."

"Yes. And, of course, we provide any continuing medical treatment that's required. I'm sure you've seen our hospital, farther up the mountain."

"What kind of medical treatment do you provide?"

"The best, but standard—if there is such a thing. We're not a *medical* research facility, Veil; this is psychological research. Lazarus People, naturally, don't require medical treatment, unless they become ill from something else while they're here. As for the others, they've already run through the gamut of medical treatment by the time they get here. They come here to share their deaths with us, Veil, not to look for a cure. There's nothing more that medicine can do for them, except make them more comfortable."

"And what you've just described to me is all that's happening on this mountain?"

Sharon flushed slightly. "Well, 'all that's happening' isn't exactly the way I'd choose to put it, but I suppose the answer to your question is, yes—that's it. It's a terribly complex field of study, but our procedures are simple. This isn't a large facility, and you've seen what I do."

"No secret research here? No Pentagon-funded studies?"

"Of course not."

"Could anyone conduct research projects here without you being aware of it?"

"You must be joking."

"Sharon, I assure you I'm not joking."

"It would be impossible. Besides, what would be the *purpose*?"

"That's what I'm asking you."

"And I've given you an answer. Veil, why are you so suspicious?"

He finished his drink and lit another cigarette. "Remember the soul-catching phenomenon you told me about?"

"Of course. It's part of the Lazarus Syndrome—but very rare."

"Is it? What you describe as soul-catching is something I've experienced all my life—or at least as long as I've been getting into serious trouble, which covers quite a few years."

There was prolonged silence as Sharon stared at him, her lips slightly parted and her eyes filled with confusion. Finally she swallowed hard and shook her head. "A bell inside your head? A chiming sound?"

"Precisely as you described it."

The woman lifted her hands in a gesture of bewilderment, let them fall into her lap. "Veil, I don't know what to say, except that I'm astonished."

"Jonathan wasn't."

"What?"

"I told Jonathan about it, during the course of one of our earlier conversations. He didn't even twitch. In light of what you've told me about Lazarus People and soul-catching, I would have thought he might have said something when I mentioned it."

"I would have thought so too," Sharon said softly, staring at the wall over Veil's left shoulder. "I'll have to ask him about it."

"I'd appreciate it if you'd hold off on that. I'd like to talk to Jonathan about it—in my own time and in my own way."

Sharon thought about it, finally nodded. "All right. Jonathan must have had a good reason. . . ." Her words trailed off as she half turned in her chair and stared into the shadows in a corner of the room.

"Sharon, I almost died at birth. Could that make me a Lazarus Person?"

The woman looked back and slowly blinked, as if she were having trouble concentrating on Veil's words. "If so, it would be a first. All of the Lazarus People we've studied had the near-death experience which changed them as adolescents or adults, after they had a fully developed human consciousness and memory pattern. Did you suffer clinical death again as an adult?"

"No."

"But you've been in the kind of dangerous situation that would trigger the soul-catching response?"

"Once or twice," Veil said, suppressing a grim smile. "In any case, the fact that I almost died at birth had nothing to do with the reason why I was invited here."

"Veil, I understand your confusion," Sharon replied uncertainly. "I'm confused myself. I wish I had answers for you, but I don't. Jonathan can sometimes be . . . peculiar. He can do things for peculiar reasons. Still, nothing must happen to him. He's very special, and you don't know what it costs him to stay here."

"Meaning?"

Sharon shook her head. "Nothing," she said in a voice just above a whisper. "He's just a very special person."

"By 'here' you mean staying alive?"

"Veil, I really don't wish to discuss Jonathan in this way. It's too personal. You're the one who should talk to Jonathan if you want certain information."

"Oh, I will. Does anyone else do this kind of research?"

"Not really." Sharon was still gazing into the shadows, but her tone had lightened, as if she were happy to be leaving the subject of Jonathan Pilgrim. "Actually, I should say nobody that we know of. There have been a number of books written on the subject, but they're all in a popular or religious vein. I don't think anyone else is trying to do serious research on the subject."

Veil studied Sharon's profile for a few moments and decided that there was nothing more to be gained by pressing the woman for information. It was Jonathan Pilgrim he would have to confront for the answers he wanted, not Sharon Solow. "I'm very attracted to you," he said at last.

Sharon looked at him, smiled. "Talk about changing gears! How very direct of you, Mr. Kendry!"

"I didn't mean to embarrass you."

"You didn't embarrass me; but you also don't know the first thing about me, aside from what I do—and thanatologists don't normally attract too many suitors."

"Tell me the first thing about you."

"Ah, but I'm of the opinion that anyone who thinks she can tell you the *first* thing about herself is a fool."

"Well said."

"Do you know the first thing about you?"

"No. Not the first."

"Strange," Sharon said after studying Veil for some time. "I think you'd be much more likely to know that first thing about yourself than I would about myself."

"Self-deprecation doesn't become you."

"I'm not being self-deprecating, Veil, just truthful. How about settling for some bits of information that are in the personal top ten?"

"Excellent."

"I'm thirty-five years old and I weigh one hundred and eleven pounds—on a good day. Men tend to find me attractive."

"Indeed!" Veil responded with a laugh.

"I've never been in love—and I assume I would know if I had. I'd like to have children; I know that my time for doing that safely is running out, but I've simply never met a man with whom I wanted to have children. Oh, I've had affairs, but none of them have ever worked out. My work *is* very important to me, and it's hard for many men to accept that. One reason why Jonathan and I get along so well together is that we're truly *friends*, with nothing beyond that to complicate matters. He understands the importance of my work, and he has no sexual interest in me."

"Because he's in love with Death?"

"Veil, I never should have said that to you."

"All right. It won't be repeated."

"I think you're a very dangerous man."

"Not to you."

Sharon smiled wryly. "No? There are different kinds of danger. I'm not sure I want to feel the things I could feel for you. From what I've observed in other people, those feelings can hurt a great deal."

Veil reached across the table and rested his hands on the table, palms up. After a second's hesitation, Sharon put her hands in his. "Many years ago a fat fortune-teller warned me that I would die at a time in my life when I was happy. At the time he said it, I really didn't pay any attention; I didn't even understand what he meant, although I thought I did then. Only recently, within the past few years, have I come to understand that, in my entire life, I've never been at peace or happy. *Excited*, yes; exhilarated, yes. But not those other things. Now I'd like to know what it feels like to be at peace and happy. I believe you're the person who can show me."

"Wow," Sharon said, smiling and raising her eyebrows. "If that's a line, it's a terrific one."

Veil laughed. "No line."

"I take it you don't believe in fat fortune-tellers."

"Oh, I believe in this one. He's very good. Also, he has a way of making his own predictions come true. But then, nobody lives forever. In fact, there's no guarantee that either of us will be alive five minutes from now, much less tomorrow or next week."

"True. Perhaps that's the real reason why I'm here."

"A number of things have happened to me since I came here."

"Now I think it's *my* turn to say 'indeed'!" Sharon replied with a thin smile. "I wish I knew what they were."

"One of the most significant things—to me, at least—is the emotional response I get when I look at you. I used to think that I wasn't afraid of death. Now I'm beginning to understand that the feeling of fear never even entered into it; I never even *thought* about death. There's a big difference."

"A serious contemplation of death can change life. That's what near-death studies are all about."

"I understand—now. I also understand that you can't experience fear without thought, and you can't display courage without fear as a backdrop. Now I'm afraid to die because I have something to lose—a newfound sense of wonder, if you will, at all these new feelings wiggling around inside me. My fat fortune-teller is turning out to be a lot smarter—and crueler—than I once thought, and he's not exactly the kind of man you underestimate. My death isn't the point, although he'll try to see to it that it happens when the time is right. I think what he really wants is for me to discover that I'm a coward as a kind of going-away present."

Sharon's hands had begun to tremble. "Veil, this 'fat fortune-teller' is a real man, isn't he?"

"Indeed. Very clever, very nasty. And now I'm the one who's talking too much."

"Veil, please. I want to know more."

"I don't think so, Sharon."

"You know you're not a coward."

"On the contrary, I know nothing of the kind. Now that I know what it means to be afraid, I have to discover if I truly have courage. I find the prospect intriguing."

"Veil—"

"No more on that, Sharon," Veil said, squeezing her hands gently. "If you'd like, you may consider this an invitation."

Sharon frowned slightly, squeezed back. "To what?"

"Perhaps to tango on the edge of time—since time, in one way or another, is beginning to shape up as the thing that links me to all this. I have a valuable adviser, of sorts; it's a dreaming state, which I don't want to get into right now. Lately my adviser has been strongly hinting that what I am, and what I have been in the past, are the keys that could open a number of locks around this place. Now I want to know more about me. My invitation is to dance with me on that edge, to see what we have to say to each other—to *feel* to each other—about our own humanity. For some reason, questions like that have become very important to me since I arrived here; more important than anything else."

"I don't know what 'locks' you're talking about," Sharon said softly, "but I do know that the edge of time is death. From the little you've told me, it seems that you're the one who's in danger of being pushed over that edge."

"Which is why I choose to be so direct."

"Veil, I don't want your fat fortune-teller's prophecy to come true."

"I'm sure he'd be highly amused if he could hear this conversation; also, probably pleased as hell with himself."

"That's what worries me."

"It shouldn't. It's my worry."

"This is a little fast for me," Sharon said, gently easing her hands away from Veil's and rising from the table. "Which is not to say that I'm turning down your offer—your invitation. As I mentioned. I've also been feeling under a bit of time pressure lately."

Veil stood up, smiled. "All right," he said evenly.

"We'll see what we shall see."

"Yes."

"Good night, Veil."

"Good night."

Chapter 12

Veil dreams.

Colonel Bean visits him in the stockade on the twenty-sixth day of his imprisonment in solitary confinement. Bean seems strangely subdued, almost sad, as he eases himself down on a metal stool in a corner of the cell and breathes a small sigh. His uniform has been freshly laundered and smells of starch. Veil, sitting on the edge of his bunk, wonders what it is that seems different about Bean, then realizes that it is the first time he has ever seen the man without tension, anger, or frustration twisting the muscles in his face. The army officer is the first visitor Veil has had since he staggered out of the jungle and turned himself in to the Military Police.

"You don't look cured to me," Bean says with a slight shake of his head. The expression on his face and his tone of voice are not unkind.

"Cured of what?"

"Whatever it was that made you pull that damn fool stunt. Jesus H. Christ, Kendry, do you realize what you could have had if you'd just gone along and done what you were told to do? The war was over for you, and you were coming out of it a hero. You were about to become a media superstar, and that's the kind of attention that makes men rich and powerful. If you'd stayed in the Army, you almost certainly would have made general. If you'd left, you would probably have been elected to office. You'd have been sitting as comfortable as a pig in shit for the rest of your life. You threw it all away."

"What do you want, Colonel?"

"It would have made things one hell of a lot simpler if you'd died in that helicopter crash."

"Sorry to inconvenience you."

"You may wish you'd died."

"I doubt it."

"What happened up there, Kendry?"

"Don't you know?"

"Some of it. I'd like to know the whole story."

"There isn't much to tell," Veil says with a shrug in his voice. "There was no attack. Cheshire Cat had been aborted."

"Of course it had been aborted. What did you expect? Madison called it off."

"Something he'd told me he couldn't do."

"Neither Madison, ARVN, nor the United States were taking orders from you, Kendry," Bean snaps, anger flaring in his voice. "I've never much cared for Madison, and I sure as hell didn't care for the stunt he pulled with Po, but it was his prerogative to do that. You seemed to be under the impression that you were a member of the Joint Chiefs of Staff."

Veil says nothing.

"Madison was telling the truth at the time he spoke to you," Bean continues, his anger gone. "He couldn't have aborted Cheshire Cat just because you wanted him to. The operation had to be called off after he told Joint Command that our newly minted war hero was on his way to fight on the side of the enemy against our allies. Who shot you down?"

"Pathet Lao."

"From your village?"

"Sure."

"You poor son of a bitch."

"They knew about Cheshire Cat; they probably learned about it five minutes after ARVN cut the orders. There were enough Pathet Lao in and around that village to fill Yankee Stadium. Po and his commandos would have had their asses shot off."

"That doesn't change the meaning of what you did, Kendry."

"I wasn't implying that it did. You asked me what happened."

"You must feel like a real loser."

"Do I, Colonel?"

"No," Bean replies after a long pause. He bows his head slightly and clasps his hands together. "I'm regular Army, Kendry. I believe in honest soldiering and honest combat. I don't go for this spy shit, and I don't go for renegades like you. If you hadn't been CIA from your training days, I'd have booted you out of this man's army a long time ago. I believe in soldiers following orders, no matter what. Now, having said that, I also want to say that I can't find the words to describe how much pleasure it gave me to learn that you'd beat the shit out of that fucking pig. I came here to tell you that I admire you for what you did—everything you did. I wouldn't have been man enough, Kendry. This Army colonel salutes you."

Veil is surprised. He stares at Bean, but the officer continues to gaze at the floor. "Thank you," Veil says simply. "I know how much it must rip your guts to say that."

"You weren't a good soldier, Kendry. Never. You were always a free-lancer, a renegade, but you were just too damn good at the things you did for us to do anything but use you. Still, soldiers follow orders, and not a single commanding officer you've ever served under ever knew what you were going to do or say from one minute to the next. You were a shit soldier, Kendry, but the finest warrior I've ever known. You were always too much of a free spirit to suit Madison, and he took it personally. He always felt the need to break you. He didn't have to put Po in that village."

"I know that."

"He had a pretty goddam good idea of what would happen; he wanted to rub your face in shit."

"I know that too. I can stand the smell of shit; what I couldn't stand was the fact that Madison was perfectly willing to sacrifice an entire village of brave people just so he could rap my knuckles."

"Well, you sure as hell rubbed *his* face in shit. But you're going to pay a hell of a cost."

"Am I, Colonel?"

"You haven't received the tab yet, Kendry. You think they're simply going to lock you away for twenty years, or maybe shoot you."

"Colonel, I haven't given a thought to what's going to be done to me. It isn't important."

"I believe you, but you'd better listen up, anyway. Madison has convinced everyone that the best thing to do with you is simply to cut you loose."

Veil feels a tightening in his stomach muscles. "Cut me loose?"

"You've got it. The Army and the politicians just want to forget you, and they can't forget you unless *everyone* forgets you. If you're stashed away in Leavenworth, some damn reporter is going to insist on knowing why. It's a story that can never be told, because this fucking war has already produced enough foolish stories about the United States Armed Forces; it may take decades for the Army to recover from what the politicians and the press have done to us. The solution is that your little session with Madison and your helicopter flight never happened. They're—we're—going to strip you of all your decorations, and your service record will be altered to cover it. You're getting bad paper—in this case a medical discharge as a loony."

"It sounds like a good plan."

"Oh, it is. Madison is very logical and very persuasive. He also has his own angle, naturally."

"Naturally."

"That fucker and I don't agree on many things, Kendry, but we do tend to agree on matters where you're concerned. Madison wants to destroy you, and he sees this as a way of doing it. He believes that the razor edge in you that makes you such a fine warrior is precisely what will gut you in civilian life. He thinks there's a good chance you'll end up a junkie, an alcoholic, or dead in some alley. I'm afraid he may be right."

"He told you this?"

"In so many words, yes. Hell, he wants you to know. He knew I'd tell you this, which is why he's using me as an errand boy to deliver a more official message."

"Which is?"

"Keep a low profile, by which I mean bury yourself someplace up to your eyeballs. If any reporters do track you down, refer them to the Pentagon. If you try to stir up old memories, the Army will come down on you. Hard. If they have to, they'll just see to it that you're put away—which was the original plan, anyway, until Madison unrolled his tongue. They'd like you to change your name."

"No."

"Kendry, they won't hassle you if you don't hassle them."

"Put me away or cut me loose, as you please," Veil replies evenly. "In either case, I'll do as I please. As a matter of fact, I'll keep the family secrets because I have no inclination not to."

Bean nods slightly, then rises to his feet. "From you, I suppose that has to be considered a major concession." He walks to the door of the cell, signals for the guard, then turns back. "An added word of warning, Kendry—personal, and definitely unofficial. I don't think it matters to Madison whether you keep your mouth shut or produce your own television program about what happened. You managed to put his ass in a sling along with your own, and he's a mite pissed at you."

Veil smiles. "Somehow that doesn't surprise me."

Bean returns Veil's smile, and for a moment there is a feeling of genuine warmth and friendship between the two men. Then Bean's smile fades. "No matter where you go, and no matter how much time goes by, you watch out for Madison and his men. If you don't end up a junkie, an alcoholic, or dead, Madison could get a little impatient."

"Thank you for the warning, sir."

Bean salutes. "Good luck to you, warrior."

Veil leaps to his feet, braces, and snaps a return salute. "Good luck to you, sir."

Chapter 13

Veil squatted on the lip of a ledge beside a cascading waterfall and used both hands to shield his eyes against the mid-morning sun as he gazed east toward the high, valley-wide wall and barbed-wire barriers that marked the entrance to the Army compound. Flanked by sheer cliffs, the compound appeared impregnable.

Veil rose, turned to go back up the trail leading to his chalet, and was startled to find Perry Tompkins leaning against a boulder a few yards away, studying him. Veil was even more surprised that the man had been able to come up behind him without his being aware of it. The burly painter with the huge, black, smouldering eyes was dressed in cut-off jeans, a T-shirt, hiking boots, and heavy wool socks. His face, arms, and legs were burned a ruddy cordovan color from the sun.

"Veil Kendry," Tompkins announced casually, a bemused

smile playing around the corners of his mouth. "In a black wig. I thought it was you lurking around here the past couple of days. You don't belong here. What the hell are you up to, pal?"

He'd always wanted to meet Perry Tompkins, Veil thought wryly, an artist whose appetite for life, artistic technique, and breadth of vision astounded him, along with most of the art-conscious people in the world. However, now—wearing a ridiculous wig and in a place where no guest could know his identity—was not the time. He lowered his head, mumbled something about mistaken identity, then started up the trail. As he came abreast of Tompkins, a huge hand reached out and gripped his shoulder.

"What are you doing here, Kendry?" Tompkins continued. His voice was low and menacing.

Veil stopped walking, but did not look up. "Back off," he said softly.

"Dr. Solow says you're on her staff. She thinks you're working for her, which is bullshit; obviously, she doesn't know who you really are. I do. We don't like our privacy invaded, Kendry. Some of us—especially me—might take great offense at your snooping around here."

Suddenly Tompkins grabbed for Veil's wig. Veil pushed away the hand, then blocked the left uppercut that followed. He stepped back and looked at Tompkins, who was staring in disbelief at his left fist, as if it had betrayed him.

"Back off," Veil repeated in the same soft tone. Deciding that his disguise was useless, at least as far as Perry Tompkins was concerned, he removed the wig from his head and stuffed it in the back pocket of his jeans. He took off his dark glasses, put them in the breast pocket of his shirt. "I don't want to fight you, Tompkins."

Tompkins met Veil's gaze. His lips curled back in a sardonic smile, and he slowly nodded with respect. "You know, you could probably hurt me if you wanted to. Not too many men can. The article implied that you were a tough bastard; at least I know you're fast."

"What article? How do you know who I am?"

"I may be responsible for your being here, and I hope I'm not going to regret it. If you're fucking over Pilgrim and Dr. Solow, you may have to hurt me. Does Dr. Solow know who you really are?"

"Yes."

"Why are you here, on this mountain?"

"That's none of your business."

"I told you we take our privacy very seriously. That's our business. And if you're trying to put something over on the people who run this place, I'll take it as my business."

"Pilgrim knows I'm here, and why."

"You looking for somebody?"

"No. Not a guest."

"Working for a newspaper or magazine?"

"No."

"I know you're a private detective. You could have been paid to snoop around here."

"I'm not a detective, private or otherwise."

"You spend a lot of time acting like one. You're acting like one now."

"I paint for money, and sometimes I help people in exchange for other things I need. I have no license. Tell me how you know who I am."

"You tell me what you're doing here."

"It has nothing to do with you, or any other guest at the hospice. I'm not invading anyone's privacy, and I'm not putting anything over on Pilgrim or Dr. Solow. I'd take it as a great courtesy if you'd mind *your* business, not tell anyone who I am, and get out of my way."

Suddenly Tompkins's great black eyes grew wider and brighter. The muscles in his massive shoulders and arms rippled as he clenched his fists. "*Damn*, Kendry, I can't remember the last time I had a good fight. How about showing me just how mean a bastard you are?"

"I won't fight you, Tompkins."

Now the eyes glinted dangerously. "Why not? You think because I'm dying I can't still kick ass like I used to?"

"That's not the point. I've got better things to do."

Tompkins, moving more carefully this time, stepped forward and flicked a left jab. Veil casually moved his head to one side and let the punch fly past his ear as he kept his eyes on the painter's right fist, which immediately flashed toward his midsection. Veil could easily have blocked, parried, or stepped out of the way, but at the last moment he decided to take the punch. He braced, tensed his stomach muscles, and hissed softly to focus his *chi* at the moment the fist landed in his stomach. The force of the blow pushed Veil back a step, but he used even this involuntary motion to advantage, reaching out to grab Tompkins's wrist and pulling his off-balance opponent after him. Veil reversed his direction, stepped around behind Tompkins, and brought the burly man's arm up behind his back in a hammerlock. With his left hand he reached into Tompkins's armpit and pressed a nerve that effectively paralyzed the painter's left side.

"I repeat," Veil said, his voice hoarse from the effort of absorbing the pain from Tompkins's blow, "I'm not here to spy on or embarrass anyone at the hospice, and I'd appreciate it if you'd keep this encounter to yourself. If and when the time is right, I'll seek you out and explain what I can to you. Under other circumstances, I'd consider it a great honor for you to allow me to sit down and talk with you. I can't begin to tell you how much I admire and respect you and your work. Just trust me for now, Tompkins. And find somebody else's ass to kick."

Veil released Tompkins's arm, turned, and headed up the trail.

"Kendry!"

Veil stopped and turned back. Tompkins was standing in the middle of the trail, thick legs slightly apart, hands extended toward Veil in a kind of gesture of supplication. His incredibly expressive eyes were filled with pain and yearning that Veil sensed were spiritual and had nothing to do directly with whatever disease was ravaging his body. "What is it?" Veil asked tightly.

"Fight me, Kendry. Please."

Veil kicked off his boots, removed his belt and shirt, and

started back down the trail toward Tompkins. This time Tompkins rushed at him like a bull, head down and arms extended out to his sides to grab and maul. Veil waited until the last moment, then took a step to his right, flexed his knees, and came up hard with his left shoulder into Tompkins's left side. The force of Veil's blow combined with Tompkins's momentum sent the big man hurtling into the air at an angle, like a train that had been derailed. Tompkins flipped in the air and landed hard on his back. For a few seconds Veil was afraid he had hurt the other man, but Tompkins had only had the wind knocked out of him. Eventually the man got to his feet and coughed. He took a deep breath, let out a whoop of delight, and charged.

Laughing along with Tompkins, Veil switched from judo to classic karate and aikido techniques, softening and symbolizing the blows but punctuating each strike at the eyes, throat, groin, spine, neck, and solar plexus with a soft hiss to let the other man know that he had been hit. Occasionally he would strike Tompkins a hard, if harmless, blow, for he sensed that the man needed physical pain to drive away, if only for a few moments, his other, more desperate pain.

However, Tompkins's huge fists connected on more than one occasion. With Veil pulling his punches and concentrating on not accidentally hurting the other man, it was inevitable that Tompkins would land a punch from time to time. Finally, with blood running into his eyes and his body sore from pounding, Veil again used judo to flip Tompkins into the air and on his back with more force than he had used before.

"Enough," Tompkins panted when he was finally able to sit up. "Thanks, Kendry. I hope I didn't hurt you too badly."

Veil threw back his head and laughed. Adrenaline was still coursing through his system, making him feel good, intoxicating him. "You're welcome, and you damn well *did* hurt me. But I enjoyed it. If you'd like, we'll do it again when I have the time."

"I'll be long dead before I'm ready for another tussle with you, Kendry," Tompkins said casually. "You're too fucking good for me."

"I'm sorry, Tompkins."

"About what?"

"The fact that you're dying."

"Yeah, me too. Dying's a pain in the ass."

"I can imagine."

"Anyway, I needed to get rid of some venom. You pulled my fangs for me, then stuck them up my ass. You have no idea how god-awful *mellow* it is around this place, what with Lazarus People who wouldn't get excited if the mountain fell on them, and future stiffs like me. It's been driving me crazy. It felt damn good to fight, yell, punch, and bleed a little." Tompkins sighed and held out his hand for Veil to pull him to his feet. "You drink?"

"I've been known to on occasion."

"Good," Tompkins said, putting an arm over Veil's shoulder and steering him off on a trail leading to the right. "I may not be able to outfight you, but I know damn well I can outdrink you."

"Well, it will certainly be interesting to see how well your massive ego survives two crushing defeats in one day."

Veil, showered and draped in a thick terry-cloth robe that was two sizes too big for him, raised his glass to Tompkins as the other man, wearing an identical robe, emerged from the bathroom. "You certainly don't fight like a man who's dying."

"Lymphatic cancer," Tompkins replied evenly as he poured himself a tumbler of Jack Daniel's over ice. "I've got another five months, maybe six. In the meantime I keep in shape and try to keep going the best I can. Where did you learn to fight the way you do?"

"Here and there."

"I know a little bit about street fighting, and you didn't learn to fight like that on the streets—not even New York's streets. You must have had some pretty fine teachers."

"A few."

"You're not very talkative," Tompkins said, studying Veil as he swirled the liquid in his glass.

"Let's find something we can talk about."

Perry Tompkins laughed. "Good grief, you mean you can't even talk about where you learned to fight?"

"The Army."

"The Army. That's like saying Hemingway learned to write from his second-grade teacher." Tompkins paused, and his smile faded. "Are you sure you're not doing a number on Pilgrim and Dr. Solow?"

"Ask them."

"Do they know what you're doing?"

"Dr. Solow knows some of it, but not all. Pilgrim will confirm that I'm not up to anything that would bring harm to anyone in the hospice."

Tompkins considered Veil's answer for a few moments, then nodded absently. He seemed to have reached some kind of decision. "You've spent a lot of time eyeballing that Army compound down the valley," he said at last. "Something over there interest you?"

Now it was Veil's turn to laugh. "Perry, *you're* the one who needs a PI license! Why won't you leave it alone?"

"Because I may be able to help you," Tompkins replied seriously.

Veil slowly sipped his drink, then set the glass down on a nearby table. "How?" he asked quietly.

"You want to get in there, right?"

Veil thought about it, nodded.

"Come here," Tompkins continued, motioning for Veil to follow him out onto the cantilevered deck that overlooked the valley. He pointed to the waterfall, a quarter of a mile away. "The light isn't right now, but when it is, you can almost see through the water. I don't know how the hell you'd get down there without breaking your ass, but I do know there's the mouth of a big cave at the base, just behind the falls."

Veil studied the broad plume of cascading water, then turned and looked down the valley toward the Army compound, which he judged to be more than two miles away. "I don't understand," he said at last. "What good is a cave behind the waterfall going to do me?"

"I do a lot of walking around here; it's good for the muscle tone." Tompkins paused and tapped his foot lightly on the hardwood deck. "This mountain is limestone; it's honeycombed with caves. I know because I keep finding openings in the mountainside. I've never gone into any of them, because I'm not into darkness right now. But the mouth of that cave behind the falls is the biggest I've seen. It just occurred to me that, given enough time, patience, and the right equipment, a man might actually be able to work his way through the mountain, down the valley, and come out somewhere on the other side of that wall. For all I know, you could end up dead or in Boston, but I figured you might want to know just in case you don't come up with any better ideas."

"Thanks, Perry. Thanks very much."

Tompkins's lips drew back in a boyish grin. "Come on, Veil, tell me what's going on. We're friends now, and this is the most interesting thing that's happened to me since the doctors told me I was going to die. You can trust me."

Veil laughed. "You won't be denied, will you?"

"Aha. Remember that everyone has secrets that may be of value to someone else. I have my own. If you'll tell me what you're after, I may tell *you* something that you'll find even more interesting that the cave behind the waterfall."

"Like what?"

"You first," Tompkins replied without smiling.

"A few days ago a man tried to kill me. It's important to me to find out why that happened. It's also important to Pilgrim, because the incident occurred on the grounds of the Institute. He suggested that I use this hospice as a base of operations while I try to find some answers."

"Why not let the police handle it?"

"It's not the kind of thing the police handle well. It's personal, may have roots that go deep into my past, and is just something that I'm best equipped to deal with myself."

"This is getting more and more intriguing," Tompkins said, raising his eyebrows slightly.

"Maybe so, but I'll have to ask you to be satisfied with what I've just given you—at least for now."

"You think the answers you're looking for could be in the Army compound?"

"It's possible. Perry, you said that you were responsible for my being invited to the Institute. What did you mean?"

"Pilgrim didn't tell you?"

"I'm beginning to think there are a great many things Colonel Pilgrim hasn't told me."

Tompkins grunted. "I've been here six months. I subscribe to about a dozen art magazines, and three months ago I read an article about you in *American Artist*. The piece had photographs of you and your work. I'd never heard of you and never seen your work, but that article made quite an impression on me—to say the least. I took it to Pilgrim. He took one look at what you were doing, and I knew he was going to invite you here."

"He said so?"

"No, he didn't say so. But I knew."

"I don't understand what you're saying, Perry. Why should my work make such an impression on you? And why should it be so important to Pilgrim?"

Tompkins smiled thinly as he walked across the room to a curtained alcove. "No one else but Dr. Solow and Pilgrim has ever seen these, Veil," he said as he pulled aside the curtain to reveal a deep, three-walled alcove hung with at least two dozen oil paintings of various sizes.

Veil stared at the paintings and suddenly felt short of breath. All of the paintings resembled eerie landscapes, but no such geography had ever existed on Earth. Walls of thick, swirling gray rose up on either side of an arrow-straight strip that was the color of steel. The corridor stretched to infinity and a horizon that was a shimmering, electric blue. The steel-colored strip and horizon were dazzling in their bold brightness, but it was the brushwork in the gray that formed the walls that finally gripped the senses, as it provided the continuing theme of the paintings. If one looked directly at the gray areas, little could be discerned but the technique of the artist combining intricate, fine-line work with gobs of paint from a palette knife to produce an illusion of churning motion.

However, the brightness of the strip and horizon kept drawing the eye back to the center of the picture—and it was then that a viewer's peripheral vision began to register ghostly, many-hued shapes moving in the mist. It was work that came fully to life only when viewed out of the corner of the mind's eye; in the hands of a master like Perry Tompkins, the illusion was unrelievedly haunting and stunning in its power. In an instant Veil perceived all the things he had been doing wrong and understood what techniques he could use to correct them.

"They're beautiful," Veil whispered. He still felt as if someone were standing on his chest. He cleared his throat, spoke louder. "They're different from anything you've ever done before. But why should you want to copy my work— even if you can do it a hundred times better?"

"Ah, but I didn't say I'd been copying your work; I said I'd seen it in *American Artist*. I also said it had impressed the hell out of me, and now you understand why. For some reason I got the notion to do these things not long after I arrived here. I did one, thought it was a rather clever illusion, and put it aside in order to go back to the other things I'd been doing. This wouldn't let me go; I kept coming back to do different versions."

"Do you dream?" Veil asked, his voice hoarse and barely audible.

"Sleep like a baby. These are the visions that—for the last few months, at least—occur to me when I'm awake. At first I thought it was mental fallout from chemotherapy, but I'd been off that for weeks when I started these. Now I've been off drugs for months, and still these visions come. You do your work from dreams, don't you?"

Veil, still transfixed by the paintings, slowly nodded. "You say that Pilgrim and Dr. Solow have seen these?"

"Yes, but no one else."

"Did you show the article to Dr. Solow?"

"No—only Pilgrim. He may have shown it to her, but I have no way of knowing. He's never returned the magazine, and he asked me very pointedly not to mention the article to anyone else."

VEIL

Veil tried to think of something to say, but couldn't. It was as if he had been struck dumb by the canvases; the paintings held him like some great magnet that was pulling his soul apart and threatening to suck him down the endless corridor and into one of the swirling gray walls where he would disappear forever. He became dimly aware of Tompkins standing beside him, pressing a glass into his hand. He raised the glass to his lips, drank all of the Scotch.

"Rather interesting, isn't it?" the dying artist continued dryly. "As far as I know, you and I are the only two people in the world who independently ended up painting virtually identical landscapes of a place that doesn't even exist."

Chapter 14

There were no locks on any door in the hospice.

Shortly after two A.M. veil entered the building housing Sharon's offices. He closed the door behind him and switched on the flashlight he had found in the utility closet in his chalet. Aiming the beam at the floor, he walked around the computer, which he did not know how to operate, and went to the bank of filing cabinets placed against the far wall. He pulled open the *A* drawer and selected a folder at random to see what it contained. It was the file of a woman by the name of Hilda Amery, a Lazarus Person who had been at the hospice for a four-week period two years before. Her file consisted of the transcript of an intake interview conducted by Sharon, a number of lengthy anecdotal reports by and about the woman, and a record of the dying she had counseled.

Veil checked a few other files and found them essentially the same, with medical histories and treatment records added to the files of those men and women who had come to the hospice to die.

Next he pulled open the *P* drawer. He quickly scanned the name tags, but did not find what he was looking for. He was about to close the drawer when, on an impulse, he pushed the hanging files forward on their metal tracks and shone his light into the bottom of the drawer. A sealed manila envelope was wedged beneath the folders. Resting the flashlight on top of the cabinet, he took out the envelope and tore it open. Inside was a single, unlabeled tape cassette.

Veil searched through the drawers beneath the computer console until he found a portable cassette player. He inserted the tape cartridge and turned on the machine, then switched off the flashlight and sat down in the darkness to listen.

"Mark. Project code: Lazarus. Subject number fifty-three. Assigned cross-reference index number—"

"Don't assign this an index number, Sharon."

Jonathan Pilgrim's voice sounded curiously distant and flat, as if he were extremely fatigued.

"You don't want me to put this in the computer?"

"Not yet . . . not until I say so. In fact, I don't even want a transcript made. Squirrel the tape away someplace safe."

"I don't understand what you're doing, Jonathan."

"I want to go on record, Sharon, but I'm not quite ready to go public. This way, if anything happens to me, you'll at least have the history of one more Lazarus Person to work with. Just go ahead and use the questions on the standard questionnaire; that will make it easier to transcribe and punch into the computer when the time comes."

"Why now, Jonathan? Is something the matter?"

"Nothing's the matter."

"You sound so tired."

"I am tired. I don't mind admitting it."

"Do you want me to get something for you from the pharmacy?"

"No. That stuff screws up my head, and I need all my wits about me for the next few weeks. I have someone coming in who may need a bit of handling. He doesn't know it, but he could make an incredibly important contribution to our understanding of the phenomena associated with the Lazarus Syndrome. I believe he represents a link we've never seen before."

"Then he's coming here to the hospice?"

"No. He'll be with me on the other mountain."

"Why?"

"Because I don't want him to know what I'm doing; at least not right away."

"Who is it?"

"I don't want to identify him to you, Sharon. If things work out, you'll understand why."

"I think I already know why. You don't want me to have any preconceptions if and when I do meet him."

"That's part of it. The fact of the matter is that I don't know all that much about him myself. Henry's out in the field now doing a work-up on his background."

"Jonathan, you're not thinking of . . . going away, are you?"

Sharon's tone had become anxious, and it was some time before Pilgrim answered.

"No. Not yet. Please ask the questions, Sharon."

"Jonathan, I don't know where to begin with you. My God, you *are* the Lazarus Project, and I know you have things to say that you've never even told me. How can I use the standard questionnaire?"

"This is just for the computer model. I'm writing up my own anecdotal report; in fact, I've been working on it for some time. It's kept in a place where you'll easily find it if anything happens to me."

"Jonathan—?"

"Come on, Sharon, let's get to it."

Sharon sighed, and there was the sound of papers being shuffled.

"Name?"

"Pilgrim, Jonathan James."

"Age?"

"Forty-eight."

"Citizenship?"

"American."

"Place of birth?"

"Boston, Massachusetts."

"Parents living?"

"Yes."

"Siblings?"

"One sister, living."

"Education?"

"Undergraduate work at Syracuse, graduate work at Massachusetts Institute of Technology. I have a doctorate in mechanical engineering."

"Profession?"

"United States Air Force, retired. I'm currently the Director of the Institute for Human Studies."

"Religion?"

"None."

"Do you believe in a personal god at this time?"

"No."

"Did you ever believe in a personal god?"

"As a child, perhaps, but not since my early teens."

"Do you believe in an afterlife at this time?"

"Skip this part, Sharon."

"Jonathan?"

"Please, Sharon. I have my reasons. Anything we don't deal with here will be in my report."

"Is your family religious?"

"My parents are lifelong Presbyterians. My sister recently converted to Baha'i."

"Did you have a religious upbringing?"

"My parents took me to church every Sunday when I was a child, but I can't say it ever had any real effect. I just never took much interest in religious matters."

"You've suffered what is known as 'clinical death'?"

"Yes."

"How long were you in this state?"

"I don't know. I was pronounced DOA at the base hospital,

but they revived me in the emergency room about three minutes after I wheeled in. I have no way of knowing how long I was dead before I got to the emergency room."

"What were the circumstances of your death?"

"Plane crash."

"Did you have what you would describe as an 'out-of-body experience'?"

"Yes."

"When were you first aware that you were outside your body?"

"Just before I got to the hospital."

"What were your surroundings?"

"The ambulance was just pulling into the driveway outside the emergency room entrance. I was floating along outside the ambulance, looking in at my body through one of the windows. I was a mess; somehow I knew I was dead."

"You didn't find this a contradiction?"

"No—not at the time. Now I do."

"What was your first reaction?"

"My first reaction was, 'Oh, shit.'"

Both Sharon and Pilgrim laughed.

"You said this aloud?"

"I thought it."

"Were you angry? Afraid?"

"None of those things. It was just 'Oh, shit.'"

"Did you feel any other presence with you?"

"No. I was alone."

"Were you lonely?"

"No, just alone. I felt no real emotion in that state."

"Were you in physical pain?"

"Quite the contrary. I felt great. There was a distinct feeling of sensual physical pleasure. If I had to describe it in words, I'd say it was like the feeling you get after a heavy workout and a shower, or after you'd made love. It was also like *being* in love with someone in whom you place total confidence and trust. In fact, I remember thinking: 'Death is Love.'"

"That's fascinating, Jonathan. You've never talked about

this before. All of the Lazarus People use almost exactly the same words to describe the feeling, but they're never quite sure what they mean by them."

"Mmm."

"What happened then?"

"I didn't want to go into the hospital. I knew—or my body did—that I was dead, and I was doing just fine wherever I was. I suspected that the doctors might try to revive me, and I was afraid of that. I'd lost my eye, and my left hand had been crushed. I knew I'd suffer terribly if they brought me back, and I didn't want that. I was whole where I was, and I wanted to stay that way. So I flew away."

"What were the mechanics of this flight?"

Again Pilgrim laughed.

"You mean, did I flap my arms?"

"Yes, I guess that is what I mean. *Did* you flap your arms?"

"No. There were no mechanics. To will it was to do it."

"But there was an actual sensation of flight?"

"Definitely."

"What direction did you go in? Up? Down? To the side?"

"I can't answer that, Sharon. Direction is a concept that had no meaning there, so I won't try to assign it a meaning here. I just went away."

"Did you see anything?"

"A huge rectangle of light. I remember thinking that it was a gate; that was the word I assigned to it because I knew there was something on the other side."

"Anything before the gate?"

"Just the color blue . . . a sea of blue. I was at once a part of that sea and something moving through it."

"Did you have any sense of time passing? Can you say how long it took you to get to the light?"

"Time had no meaning."

"All right. What happened then?"

"In the hospital?"

"At the gate of light. Could you see beyond it?"

"No. It was too bright."

"How big was it?"

"No meaning."

"Was there anything or anybody in or near the gate? Say, a robed figure?"

"No."

"Voices?"

"No."

"Any sound at all?"

"No. There was absolute silence. There's no silence here to compare with it."

"Did you have any feelings at this time?"

"Ecstasy."

"Did you want to go through the gate?"

"Yes. Definitely."

"Did you?"

"No. I returned to the hospital and went back into my body."

"Did you feel hands pushing you, or voices urging you to go back?"

"No. It was a voluntary act."

"If what you were experiencing was so pleasant, why did you choose to return to what you knew would be agony?"

There was a considerable pause before Pilgrim finally answered.

"I was curious."

"Weren't you curious about what might be on the other side of the gate?"

"Yes, but I knew that the gate would always be there waiting for me. On the other hand, I was afraid that I wouldn't have the option of returning once I went through it. Knowing it was there gave me courage. I decided to come back here, at least for a while, and see how things turned out."

"So? How have things 'turned out'?"

"Sharon, I'm still working on the answer to that one—as you well know."

"Yes, I do know. In general, how do you feel now?"

"Well, you're aware of all my medical problems. I have a lot of problems with fatigue. Emotionally, I feel . . . distanced."

"Can you expand on what you mean by 'distanced'?"

"I'll try. What I mean is that I find myself constantly amazed—and amused—by some of the things most people take seriously. I used to be known as a man with an extremely quick temper. Now I rarely get angry at anything."

"What you're describing sounds like apathy."

"But it isn't. In fact, I have a much greater sense of wonder and involvement with the world as a whole. It's just much harder to get angry about anything. I think the strongest and most consistent feeling I have is curiosity."

"About what?"

"Everything. Especially us—human beings."

"Are there things you took seriously before the accident that you don't take seriously now?"

"Any number of things, but I don't see any need to list them. The point is that you become more curious and involved, but less emotional. At least I did."

"All Lazarus People do, Jonathan. You know that."

"Compiling statistics is your job."

"I can't argue with that. Once again, there was no religious feel to any of this?"

"None."

"Have you experienced any unusual physical sensations since your near-death experience?"

"Ghost-limb syndrome, but that's to be expected after any amputation. It often feels like my hand is still there."

"Jonathan, that's about it for the questionnaire. Is there anything you want to add?"

"No."

"Are you sure, Jonathan? I'm a little worried about you."

"I'm sure, and there's no need for you to worry about me. Remember that I'm still waiting to see how things turn out."

"You really believe that this man you've invited to the Institute can give you the answer, don't you?"

"Let's close this out, Sharon. I really am tired."

"All right, Jonathan. End of intake interview. Mark."

Chapter 15

"Veil? Can't you tell me what this is all about?"

Veil glanced at Sharon, who was studying him from where she sat at the far end of the conference table in her suite of offices. There was confusion and hurt in her pale, silver-streaked eyes, and she was staring at him as if he were a stranger—a reaction Veil found perfectly understandable, since he had been going out of his way to behave like a stranger. Something about the atmosphere surrounding the Institute, and particularly the hospice, was very disorienting to him, he thought. There was not only the mystery of the Golden-Boy to be solved, but also a mystery within himself—a riddle that had only posed itself since he'd agreed to be Jonathan Pilgrim's guest. It was as if there were something in the air over these two particular mountains that made him open and trusting in ways he had never before been in his life. Now he felt betrayed, not only by Pilgrim—and possibly by

Sharon and Henry Ibber—but also by his own instincts. He had been wandering around in a mental fog, displaying the kind of doe-eyed innocence that could get him killed, and he had resolved that it was going to stop.

"Veil, did you hear me?"

"Not now, Doctor."

"Doctor? We're getting rather formal all of a sudden, aren't we?"

"I want to wait until Pilgrim and Ibber get here so that I won't have to repeat myself."

"Henry will be here?"

Veil nodded. "I asked Pilgrim to bring him over."

"Veil, what's *wrong*?"

"That's what I'm trying to find out. It's time to sort out a few things."

"But—"

"Kendry?!"

Veil turned to face Henry Ibber, who had stopped just inside the door to the conference room. Ibber's high, shiny forehead glistened with perspiration, and the mouth below the drooping black mustache gaped open with astonishment.

"Come in and sit down, Ibber," Veil said curtly. It seemed that Pilgrim had not told his investigator who wanted to see him, and Veil wondered why.

Ibber's dark eyes suddenly flashed with anger. "What the hell are you doing here, Kendry? And who are you to be giving me orders?"

"Go ahead, Henry." Jonathan Pilgrim's voice, soft but insistent, came from the doorway just behind the large-framed Ibber. "Do as he asks."

Ibber thrust his stocky shoulders forward and glared at Veil for a few moments, then abruptly walked across the room and sat down at the table, next to Sharon. Pilgrim, walking casually with his hand in his pocket and a faintly bemused expression on his face, entered the room and sat down at the end of the table closest to where Veil was standing, apart from his two colleagues.

"It's your show, my friend," Pilgrim continued, turning to Veil. "Let's do it."

"We'll do it, all right, Colonel," Veil said, his voice hard. "You've been jerking me around since I got here. I don't like being 'handled,' and I want to know why you felt you had to do it. I also want to know what part you expected me to play in this spook show you've got over here."

Pilgrim glanced sharply at Sharon, who blanched and put a hand to her mouth. "The tape," she said in a husky voice. "He's heard the tape."

"You're damn right I've heard the tape. I've also had a very interesting chat with Perry Tompkins, who was kind enough to show me his latest paintings. That means it's time to tell me the name and rules of the game you've been playing."

Veil had been speaking to Sharon, but the woman was still staring wide-eyed at Pilgrim. "Jonathan, I'm so sorry. I never thought—"

"Don't worry about it, Sharon," Pilgrim said easily as he lit a cigar. "It's not your fault. I'm the one who brought him over here. I knew it was risky, but I couldn't think of any other place to put him where he'd be safe. He'd have eventually found out, anyway; hell, I'd have told him. It's just bad timing."

"My God, Jonathan. He's the one, isn't he?"

Pilgrim looked at Veil and winked broadly. "That's him."

"Come on, Sharon," Veil said. "Are you trying to tell me that you didn't know or guess? You were the first person I was supposed to see. Does the Colonel always use his director of near-death studies to conduct garden-variety interviews on the other mountain?"

"No, but—"

"I'd told her that we had a couple of people out sick," Pilgrim interrupted. "She really did just make the connection, Veil. She saw Perry's work, but she's never seen yours. You've heard the tape; I wanted Sharon to work with you because I needed her special perspective, but I didn't want her to know why. I wanted any discoveries about you to be made independently, not by somebody like me—looking for and hoping to make them."

"Excuse me," Ibber said, looking back and forth between Sharon and Pilgrim. "Would somebody mind telling *me* what this is all about?"

"Sorry, Henry," Pilgrim said with a shrug. "I'm afraid your time is being wasted. Veil was quite insistent that I include you in this meeting, so I brought you over. I don't think he'd have believed me if I told him that you didn't have the slightest notion of why I really wanted him here."

"Your real reason for wanting me here isn't the point, Colonel. Somebody tried to kill me, remember?"

"I remember," Pilgrim replied softly.

Veil turned to face the Institute's chief investigator. "Ibber's the man who ran my background check."

"Just a minute, Kendry!" Ibber shouted as he leapt to his feet. "Are you accusing me of something?"

"You'll know when I accuse you of something," Veil said without emotion.

"I checked you out the same as I do, or someone on my staff does, every other individual who's invited to the Institute. I wrote up my report and submitted it to Jonathan. Period."

"You knew that the man who tried to kill me was a Mamba—an Army assassin."

"So what? That was none of my business."

"Then what were you doing there when Parker questioned me?"

"Parker wanted another witness. In case you didn't notice, he and Jonathan don't get on too well."

"Jonathan?" Sharon's voice was trembling. "What is all this talk about killing?"

The Institute's director removed the cigar from his mouth and pointed it like a spear at Veil's chest. "It's still Mr. Kendry's show; let him direct it the way he wants."

Veil felt the first stirrings of doubt, and he frowned slightly as he studied Pilgrim's face. "They really didn't know about your plans for me, did they?"

Pilgrim grunted softly. "Now you've got it. I'm curious as

to what it is you think you know. Do you believe that one of us is responsible for the attack on you? All of us?"

"Make your point, Kendry," Ibber said in a voice still heavy with anger.

Veil wheeled on the investigator. "Did you find anything in my background that you thought was particularly interesting?"

"As a matter of fact, I did. I suspected that your military record had been doctored, and I included that in my report. Again, so what? Picking up on things like that is what I'm paid to do."

"Did you tell anybody else?"

"Why should I tell anybody else? What the hell makes you think you're so goddam important, Kendry? As far as I was concerned, you were just another subject for investigation."

"You didn't know that your boss really wanted me here as part of near-death studies?"

"I don't have anything to do with near-death studies, Kendry. This is the first time I've ever even set foot on this mountain. And I *still* don't know that what you say is true. All I hear is you talking."

"It's true," Pilgrim said, his voice flat and slightly distant. "In fact, I *have* been running a game on Veil, and he has every right to be upset. His mistake is in thinking that there's some connection between that game and another problem he and I have to deal with. He's wrong, and I think he's beginning to see that. In fact, it wouldn't surprise me to find him willing to let the two of you go on now about your own business."

"I'd prefer to stay," Ibber announced as he abruptly sat down in his chair. "Kendry dragged me over here, and now I think I have the right to know what's going on."

"Henry," Sharon said quietly, touching the investigator's arm, "I really think we should both go."

"It's all right, Sharon," Pilgrim said casually. "Half my cat's hanging out of the bag, anyway, so we may as well all hear Veil drag out the rest of the beast. Assuming that's all right with him, of course."

"Oh, Jonathan," Sharon breathed, "it's so personal."

Ibber cleared his throat. "Jonathan, would you like us to leave?"

"I told you that was up to Veil," Pilgrim replied distantly. "He's in charge."

"Why did you want me for near-death studies, Jonathan?" Veil asked quietly, ignoring Ibber.

Pilgrim motioned for Veil to sit down at the table, but Veil shook his head. "If there's a connection between why I wanted you and that other business, I'll be damned if I know what it is," Pilgrim said easily. "I told you that."

"Why didn't you tell me you were a Lazarus Person?"

"Nobody but Sharon knew. Now, of course, you and Henry also know. The reason for my keeping it a secret is very practical. A moment ago you referred to near-death studies as a spook show—"

"I apologize for that remark," Veil said quickly, glancing at Sharon.

"No need. That would be the reaction of most people. As I've indicated to you, for now much of the Institute's prestige is linked to my personal prestige and integrity. I can't afford to be linked with a 'spook show,' even if that 'spook show' is, in my opinion, probably the most important research in which we're involved."

"Why did you feel that I had to be 'handled'? Why have you been lying to me all along?"

"Because the discovery of what you are couldn't be rushed. The moment I saw the similarity between your work and Perry's, I understood the significance. But you had to be peeled like an onion; if you were aware of what I wanted to know, it could interfere with the process."

"What *is* the significance?"

"Don't you realize it yet?"

"I've had a few other things on my mind, Jonathan. Also, frankly, I'm not sure I give a damn—not if it won't help answer the other questions I have. We've already decided that I'm not a Lazarus Person."

"And *that* is precisely what makes you so important, Veil." Excitement was beginning to hum in Pilgrim's voice. "Despite the fact that you've never had a near-death experience, except as an infant, you display most of the characteristics of Lazarus People—including the rarest trait of all, soul-catching."

Ibber started to say something, but Veil cut him off with a sharp wave of his hand. "Go ahead, Jonathan. Please."

"In many ways you act like a Lazarus Person, even though you aren't. The close rapport you've felt with me from the beginning is typical; Lazarus People tend to recognize and like one another. My guess is that the brain damage you suffered as an infant did to you what the near-death experience does to Lazarus People as adults; it literally ripped apart some psychic barrier between your conscious and unconscious states of awareness. Your dreams take you to a special place, and you've painted pictures of it."

"What about Perry Tompkins?"

"A unique case, like you—but different from you. With Perry we're dealing with a giant, a man with artistic talent and sensitivity almost beyond words. That talent—goosed, if you will, by his approaching death—is his ticket to this special place. You both travel there, but by different routes."

"What 'place,' Jonathan?"

"It's the place beyond the gate, Veil. The paintings you and Perry produced—that's exactly what it looks like. I know, because I've been there. You and Perry keep poking your heads, your collective consciousness, into a land of the soul I could only reach by dying."

Veil turned quickly toward Sharon when he heard her gasp.

"Oh, yes," Pilgrim continued, also looking at the woman. "I've been through the gate, Sharon; just one more thing I've felt the need to lie about. I still don't understand quite how, but I did manage to wrench myself back through—back here. But I was there, on the astral plane. It's where Veil and Perry travel, in their own separate ways, on the vehicle of imagination, and it's where they will go when they die."

Veil swallowed and found that his mouth was dry. "*Astral plane*, Jonathan?"

"Oh, hell!" Pilgrim snapped with more impatience than Veil had ever seen him display. "And you, of all people, wonder why I keep secrets. Call it what you will. I use the term 'astral plane'; others would call it something else. There are a thousand different names for it, I'm sure, and it's been part of humankind's collective racial consciousness since we dropped out of the trees and crawled into caves. It spawned religion, feeds art, and was the midwife of science; insistence on the quaint idea that the place must have some kind of caretaker, and disagreement over how the caretaker mows the lawn, has broken our bones, spilled our blood, and pretended to offer hope at the same time as it crushed love and life. The fact of the matter, put as simply as I can manage, is that I needed you here so that I could try to prove that heaven exists."

Chapter 16

Veil leapt into space, then spread his arms and arched his back to control the angle of his body in free-fall. As he plummeted, the thought flashed across his mind that he was diving off a hundred-fifty-foot cliff into unknown depths, had been forced to kill an American soldier who was a super-assassin as well as—probably—a double agent, was being hunted by Defense Intelligence Agency operatives, had fallen in love for the first time in his life, had discovered a bizarre personal link with one of the greatest artists who had ever lived, and was now on the first leg of a journey that could end in torture and death—all because of a likable madman's obsession and impossible quest. Nevertheless, his own quest had to continue; he could not walk away from the Institute and Jonathan Pilgrim's insanity without going into hiding, and he had rejected that alternative years before. He preferred to make his stand here, on his unknown enemy's ground.

At the last moment he ducked his head, brought his arms together, and clenched his fists to absorb the force of impact with the water. He sliced down into the cold, dark depths, reversed direction, and pulled easily toward the surface at an angle that would bring him to the surface behind the waterfall.

He came up in roaring darkness and groped forward through swirling foam until his fingers touched stone. He hauled himself up on a ledge and unstrapped the belt that secured a rolled towel to his waist. He tore away the protective layers of plastic wrap, unrolled the towel, and searched through its contents until he found his flashlight, which he turned on.

The mouth of the cave behind the falls was high but relatively shallow, an amphitheater of smooth stone from which radiated a number of smaller caves of various sizes going in different directions. There were two caves, each large enough for him to walk in, which appeared to head toward the east.

Veil set the flashlight down beside him on the ledge and sorted through the rest of the things he had brought with him; jeans and a sweater, sneakers, a dozen extra batteries, chalk, his .38, and a makeshift compass he had fashioned from cardboard, thread, and a needle he had magnetized from the motor in the refrigerator in his chalet.

He dried himself, stripped off his shorts, and dressed in the dry clothes. He rewrapped the other items in the towel, picked up the flashlight, and entered the first cave on his left.

He had gone less than two hundred yards when the cave began to narrow, then abruptly became no more than a crevice that was too narrow for him to enter. He retraced his steps to the amphitheater and entered the second cave. Twenty-five yards in, the second cave suddenly branched off into three others.

Veil stopped to take his compass and chalk from the towel, and as he put the flashlight in his armpit to free his hands the beam passed across something in the middle cave that flashed orange. Veil gripped the light and shone it down the cave, and in an instant knew that he would need neither compass nor chalk to continue his journey. He also knew that he would have to rethink his original assessment of the hospice and the people who stayed there.

Someone at the hospice—Lazarus Person, patient, or staff member—was a spy. A route that could lead only to the Army compound had already been marked; there were orange blaze marks, spaced every fifteen yards, on the walls of the cave, and scuff marks in the dust on the floor.

Veil took his .38 out of the towel and stuck it in his belt. Then he started off on the route marked by the bright orange crosses.

It had taken enormous time and effort, involving much trial and error, to mark the route, Veil thought as he glanced at his watch and found that he was into his third hour underground. The route was not direct, but involved many twists and turns in a succession of radiating caves, many of which cut off initially to the north or south. Time was something neither Lazarus People nor the dying at the hospice had much of, since both groups were, for different reasons, transient. The hospice was essentially a closed society, and not even a permanent staff member could have spent the weeks it must have taken to blaze this route without being missed—unless there had been collusion by either Sharon Solow or Jonathan Pilgrim, or both.

Or unless his original assumption had been wrong, Veil thought, and the longer he spent in the marked caves, the stronger became his conviction that this was the case. It was the Army spying on the hospice, not vice versa. Why? Death by natural causes and searching for heaven seemed unlikely topics of interest for the personnel in a top-secret military research facility.

And always the problem remained of determining who had spotted him, and why it had been quickly decided that he should be killed. What *else* was Pilgrim hiding? Veil wondered. And was it hidden at the hospice?

Twenty minutes later he felt fresh air gently wafting in his face as the cave widened and sloped sharply upward. Veil climbed up the rock slope and found himself at a fairly broad cave mouth that looked down into the valley and the rustic, wooden buildings of the military compound. The buildings were spaced in a horseshoe pattern, with a larger building set at the closed end, the open end facing inland. The enclosed area of the horseshoe was a grassy commons area crisscrossed by white gravel walks, and with a flagpole in the center. The American flag flapped in the wind blowing down the valley from the sea.

Veil put his flashlight into the rolled towel, crouched down, and wedged the bundle beneath a ledge. As he straightened up, a soft chiming sound tolled in his mind.

Danger.

But from where? The chime sound had saved his life too many times in the past for him to doubt it now, but he also did not want to retreat after coming this far. He was silently crouched just inside the mouth of the cave, trying to decide what to do next, when his decision was made for him.

"We know you're there, Kendry." The voice was deep and resonant, absolutely calm, firm with self-confidence. It came from somewhere above him, just outside the mouth of the cave; the man would be in an advantageous position, with the sun above and behind his back. "We've been waiting on you. You tripped a sensor when you entered the cave, another one when you were halfway through, and a third just now. We know what you can do, pal, and we're not going to fuck with you. If you come out of there holding anything but the air over your head, you'll be at least twenty pounds heavier by the time you hit the ground. Come on, now; step out slow and easy."

Mambas.

Veil snatched up the towel, cradled it in his belly to protect the flashlight, then dove headfirst down the sharp incline. He turned and rolled as he landed on his shoulder, then slid on his back to the bottom. There he rolled into a ball and hugged his knees as he waited for what he assumed would be a murderous hail of bullets ricocheting off the stone walls and ceiling.

Instead there was a single, hollow *phut*. Something large, not a bullet, passed through the air over his head, smacked hard against a wall, and fell to the floor. Veil cursed aloud as the gas grenade exploded.

Chapter 17

He awoke to find himself naked, in a cage that had been anchored to the ground in the commons area, near the flagpole. The cage, with a locked drop gate facing the open end of the horseshoe of buildings, was not large enough for him to stand or fully extend himself on the ground, and Veil had to shuffle on all fours in order to turn around. It was what, in Vietnam, had been called a tiger cage, or "cramper." The object of the exercise, of course, was to break down psychological defenses through steady debilitation, as well as humiliation, and a prisoner's own mind was depended upon to facilitate the process.

From the position of the sun Veil guessed that it was early morning, which meant that he had been unconscious for almost twenty-four hours. He had a throbbing headache, and his mouth tasted green.

There was a good deal of activity in the compound as Army

personnel, some with white lab coats worn over their uniforms, passed from building to building. Veil counted three women. Out on a dirt field just beyond the open end of the horseshoe and twenty yards from the bank of the swift-running river, six men in baggy black jumpsuits practiced advanced, complex martial arts *kata* under the watchful eyes of two Japanese, one young and one old. The old man, dressed in a flaring crimson robe and a broad, crimson headband, stood in front of the exercising men, erect, as still and as silent as a stone pillar. Both hands were placed on a simple wooden staff he held at arm's length in front of him. The old master was practicing his own *kata*, Veil thought, a Zen-linked exercise; without so much as the blink of an eye, the old man was able to project an aura of raw, mind-harnessed energy powerful enough to make an observer half believe that, if he so desired, the old man could drive the staff to its hilt in the ground, or perhaps split the world with an overhead blow.

With no apparent motions or words that Veil could hear, the old master was directing the *kata* of the six men moving in front of him. Fists flew, hands chopped, fingers poked, arms whirled, bodies spun. It was all done with blinding speed, a very special kind of beauty that tugged on a line between the mind, heart, and groin, and—like a deadly line of male Rockettes in a surreal Radio City Music Hall of sky, earth, water, and stone—in perfect unison.

Or almost perfect unison. Although Veil could not detect any mistakes, some were obviously made. On occasion the younger Japanese, a burly man dressed only in a loincloth, would abruptly step up behind one of the exercising Mambas and deliver a blow across the man's back or legs with a long flail of split bamboo; the force of each blow was such that the *splat* of bamboo striking flesh would echo down the valley, bouncing back and forth between the rock faces of the surrounding mountains. No struck Mamba flinched or slowed his pace; the ballet of violence, danced to the staccato, syncopated rhythm of beaten flesh, continued.

124

The point, aside from punishing errors in form, was to teach that pain is an illusion.

No one, researcher or Mamba, so much as glanced in Veil's direction. Veil turned around and leaned back against the bars. He brought his knees up to his chest, rested his head on his forearms, and waited.

Around noon, Veil felt the hairs on the back of his neck begin to tingle. He turned his head and found himself looking up at three of the Mambas and their Japanese master. The Americans had showered and changed into fresh jumpsuits, and Veil sensed that the master had brought them here to engage in some kind of mental exercise—perhaps nothing more than to test their stealth against his sixth sense, for they had approached without making a sound. The expressions on the faces of the three Americans were intense; the green eyes of the Mamba on the right, a stocky man with brown hair and a pockmarked face, gleamed with a naked yearning to test himself against Veil.

Although he stood as erect as the Americans, the Japanese now projected an aura of relaxation. His eyes were cast down—a gesture of respect.

"Good day, gentlemen," Veil said easily. "Listen, as long as you're up, would one of you do me a favor? You can never find your waiter when you want him. I'd like somebody to tell the maitre d' that I'm ready to order. Also, I'd like some water."

Once again, without any signal from the master that Veil could detect, the three Americans turned and walked away. The old man remained behind for almost a minute, eyes still cast down, then he, too, turned and walked away.

All day he had burned in the sun, and Veil knew he had lost a great deal of body moisture. Now, with the sun going down, the chill and damp of the Northern California evening was beginning to clog his lungs and seep up from the ground into his body. He shivered, and this only served to increase the spasmodic cramping of his muscles that he had been suffering since mid-afternoon. He kneaded the cramped muscles, then tried to exercise as best he could in the small cage in order to avoid hypothermia.

He heard a footfall behind him, turned, and found Colonel Parker standing over the cage, looking down at him. The setting sun shone golden on the man's hard, craggy face and made his eyes glitter. The Army officer stood with his hands behind his back, feet slightly apart. Over his shoulders was draped a heavy, cable-knit sweater, the sight of which made Veil groan inwardly.

"How're you doing, Kendry?" Parker asked in a flat voice.

"This tiger cage is a bit crude, Colonel," Veil replied hoarsely. His throat was now raw with thirst. "I'm really disappointed. From you I'd have expected nothing less than state-of-the-art."

"This is state-of-the-art, Kendry," Parker answered in the same flat voice. It was as if, safe on his home territory, he did not need to exhibit the blustering he had displayed in Pilgrim's office. Then again, Veil thought, Parker was no longer frustrated; indeed, he was beginning to look very much like a winner. "It cuts through all the bullshit. I don't know what kind of drug-resistance training you've had, and I don't care to take the time to find out. Electricity and pliers have always made me a bit squeamish. I'm an American, not a goddam torturer."

"Boy, am I glad to hear that."

"We've discovered that a bit of rolling around in your own piss and shit, combined with a great deal of thirst, usually does the trick—and with less chance of permanent damage. We're just leaving you alone and letting nature take its course. You know the routine."

"I sure do. So let's stop wasting time. Bring me a pitcher of water and tell me what you want to know."

Parker grunted. "That's good, Kendry. You have to respect a man who can make jokes while his throat and guts are turning to sand."

"What the hell makes you think I'm joking?"

Parker said nothing. Sunset gleamed in his steel-gray hair like veins of gold in rock.

"You've already wasted a day," Veil continued, his voice cracking. He coughed dryly, and pain that was not quite as severe as his desire for water flashed from his throat to his chest. "You could've come to me this morning and I'd have told you everything you wanted to know."

"Really? Then why didn't you simply come to me instead of trying to bust in here?"

"Because I had the sneaking suspicion that you'd still wring me out before you accepted anything I had to say. Also, there was no way you'd give me the guided tour of this place I need to answer my own questions. Now that you've got my ass, I have no choice but to cooperate."

"*That*, Kendry, is the truth."

"I came back to the Institute for the same reason I tried to sneak in here: I need to find out why your man wanted to kill me."

"Who are you working for? The Russians? Cuba? East Germany?"

"I'm not an intelligence agent, Parker, and I'm not working for anyone but myself. All I'm trying to do is find a way to protect my own ass."

"I'll see you tomorrow, Kendry," Parker said as he turned away.

"Parker!" Veil got up on his knees and gripped the bars of the cage with both hands. "Let me explain! Why walk away?"

"Because I haven't got time to listen to bullshit," Parker replied over his shoulder, waving his right arm in a casual gesture of dismissal. "You're just not thirsty enough. Sweet dreams, jerk."

Veil sank back down to the dank ground and watched Parker walk away toward the large building at the base of the horseshoe. His thirst and cold demanded that he call after the man, but his mind and heart told him that it would be useless to do so. Parker was not going to believe anything he had to say until Parker was certain that Veil was sufficiently—and thoroughly—broken. He was going to have to suffer.

Veil did a few isometric exercises against the bars, and the cramping in his muscles eased somewhat. He propped himself up in a corner, wrapped his arms around his legs, closed his eyes, and began a series of deep-breathing exercises in an attempt to relax and conserve energy. Whatever further ordeal lay ahead of him, he knew that he was going to need all of his reserves of strength and will to meet it. In the meantime, he was dead meat if his unknown enemy was in the compound.

He needed rest, and he needed to protect his mind as best he could. For a few hours, at least, he knew how to escape to a place that was safe and warm.

Chapter 18

Veil dreams.

Dreams within the dream.

He sits bolt upright in his broken bed, sweat-pasty sheets sticking to his bare flesh like a shroud. He instinctively grabs for his rifle, but it isn't there. After a few moments the realization comes that he is not fighting in Vietnam or Laos, but living in a summer-smothered, roach-infested studio apartment not much bigger than a closet on New York's Lower East Side. He has been in the city now for three months, working as a temporary laborer to earn money, walking the streets to fight pain. He knows he is drinking far too much. He would like to brawl, but does not for fear that he will accidentally kill somebody. He has crippled three would-be muggers, possibly killed a fourth, and he knows that he is losing his mind.

For almost a month he has been experiencing a recurring

dream—night after night, all night. The dream is not quite a nightmare, but it leaves him anxious and fearful in a way that combat never did.

In the dream he finds himself on a steel-gray path that stretches off to a horizon that is a brilliant blue and which he feels with his heart as well as sees with his eyes. Although the surface on which he stands is flat and level, he constantly fears that he will lose his balance if he takes a step in any direction. The surface has no "feel," but seems a natural extension of his own flesh.

The path is bounded on each side by walls of thick, swirling gray mist that seems to be alive; the walls hiss, although he is not sure if the sound is real or only in his mind. Figures of subtle, almost translucent color move through the mist and occasionally seem to stop and peer out at him. Some of the figures have teeth. However, he can only glimpse these moving things out of the corner of his eye, for he does not dare to look at either wall directly. He hates this fear and has never known anything like it; still, he cannot summon the courage to overcome it. Although he is deeply ashamed of his cowardice, there is no way he can bring himself to turn body or head and look at, or into, the walls.

He has come to believe that to do so, even in a dream, is to die. He will be sucked through the gray barrier, and there will be no way out.

Veil peels the sopping sheets from his skin, sits up on the edge of the bed, and buries his face in his hands. Sweat of both summer and fear slides through his fingers and drips on the floor. He is determined to find the courage to step or turn on this dream-path, even if it means his death.

But Veil does not want to die, nor does he want to go mad. Having survived in the jungles of Southeast Asia, he does not want to be killed by his own mind—nor transformed into a coward. If he cannot rid himself of the dream, Veil thinks, then he must find the courage to conquer it.

He rises, turns on the light, and goes to the indelibly stained washstand in a corner. He studies himself in the

VEIL

cracked mirror and is disgusted by what he sees. His eyes are chronically bloodshot from too much alcohol and not enough sleep, and there are dark rings under them. He feels his gut pressing against the dirty porcelain of the washbasin; the flesh of his face is sallow and puffy. He is getting soft.

He dresses in yesterday's clothes that smell of sweat and goes out to walk the streets. There is no breeze, and the night air sitting on the sidewalks is as stifling as the air in his apartment. He finds himself walking toward the West Village, purposely choosing the darkest streets and slowing as he approaches and passes alleys. He would like to be attacked so that he can fight to relieve his tension. However, stories of a strange, savage man with long yellow hair and incredible fighting skills have spread throughout the neighborhood, and Veil is not bothered.

He reaches the lights and mellow ambience of the West Village and wanders aimlessly through its streets crowded with jazz bars, coffeehouses, crafts shops, art galleries, and clinging couples. He passes an art supply shop and continues walking for almost four blocks while the seed of an idea takes root in his mind and grows to block out the sights, sounds, and smells around him.

His problem is finding the courage to turn and look directly at one of the gray walls in his dream, even if it means his death. Perhaps if he approaches the problem from a different perspective, in a different dimension; perhaps if he tries to draw or paint his dream on paper . . .

Veil returns to the shop and purchases art supplies—charcoal, drawing pencils, watercolors, brushes, oil crayons, paper—and starts home. He finds his pace quickening as his excitement builds. He has a feeling of anticipation, of being on the verge of an important discovery. For the first time since returning to the United States he is free of stress and anxiety and is actually looking forward to something. Awake, he finds that he is not afraid to deal directly with things he can only bear to glimpse peripherally in dreams.

When he arrives back at his apartment, he sits down on the splintered floor and immediately begins to work. He has no skills, no idea of the proper way to use the materials he has purchased. Frustration builds as he struggles to capture on paper the essence of what he has witnessed in sleep; he experiences anger at his clumsiness, but also feels a kind of ecstasy that takes him out of himself, beyond his distress. He works through the night and by dawn has used up all his paper.

He sleeps during the day, missing work. For the first time in many weeks he does not dream. He is awakened by a late-afternoon thunderstorm that cools the air and flushes the streets of both city and mind. A cool breeze wafts through Veil's tiny apartment as he rises and dresses. He thinks about going out to buy something to eat, but discovers that he is not hungry.

Slowly, he leafs through the drawings and paintings he has made the night before. He finds them dismayingly crude, not even an approximation of the path, walls, and horizon he has witnessed.

And so he begins again.

He does not have money to buy more paper, and so he uses the backs of the sheets he has already drawn and painted on. Completely absorbed in his task, it is not until many hours later, when he has exhausted his supplies, that Veil realizes he is actually relaxed, even happy. He is still dismayed by the inadequacy of his representations, but he is equally awed by the psychic comfort he has acquired merely through the process of struggling with his visions. This is a different kind of combat, he thinks, combat in which winning the war is not as important as waging it; it is a bloodless battle that keeps the enemies in the self at bay, and now he dares to hope that he has found a way to fight for his sanity, and perhaps even his life.

If Madison wants him dead, then Madison is going to have to kill him.

Veil showers, shaves, and dresses. He has decided that he will look for work in the village. He may even ask the owner of the art supply shop for a job, or see if, in exchange for materials and lessons on how to use them, there might not be some service he can perform.

Chapter 19

T he nerve cells in his body reacted to the icy water that splashed over him, shocking him awake, like the flame of a blowtorch. Veil's head snapped back and slammed against the bars of his cage, and he barely managed to choke off a scream as his back arched and the muscles of his burned, feverish body objected to this insult by twitching and knotting in torturous spasms. The moment he could control any movement at all, he was licking like an animal at the droplets of water on his shoulders, arms, and the backs of his hands.

"You ready to talk to me, Kendry?"

Veil raised his head and squinted up into the sun. Parker was leaning on the top of the cage, looming over him. Veil opened his mouth to speak, but only gagging sounds would issue from his dry throat and past his swollen tongue. A long-handled ladle suddenly came out of the sun and appeared in his field of vision. Veil grabbed for it, spilling half its contents onto the ground. He gripped the bowl with both hands and drank what was left; the ladle was pulled away as he sucked air. To his surprise, another ladle was offered. He drank until the bowl was empty, sighed, and rested his head against the bars. "Thank you," he managed to say.

"Don't thank me," Parker replied curtly. "You know it's still just part of the routine. I gave you just enough water to get your head straight and your vocal cords working. There's no need for you to suffer like this, and frankly, I don't much enjoy watching it. You may be in the cage, but you're the one with the key in your hand. You can open it anytime you want to. Do I have to remind you that any man can be broken?"

"You won't listen to me."

"I wouldn't listen to you before because you were getting ready to throw some bullshit in my direction. I may listen to you now. We'll see what your opening notes sound like. Tell me the truth and I'll give you all the water you want. You'll get food and medical attention. You'll get your clothes back, and you'll get out of that cage so you don't have to cook all day and freeze all night. If you *don't* tell me the truth, you're going to die right there on the ground. I swear it, Kendry. Dying of thirst isn't chicken soup, but you'll be doing it to yourself. From the looks of you, I'd say you have another night and day left in you. But you won't let it go to the end. No man could. You'll talk finally, so why not do it now and save both of us all this bother?"

Veil breathed deeply, dropped his chin on his chest, and tried to focus his thoughts through a mental haze of fever. "I tried to tell you the truth yesterday. You just walked away."

"Oh, shit, Kendry, are you going to—?"

"*Listen* to me, Parker!" Veil croaked. He swallowed hard and managed to work up some moisture in his mouth. He licked the roof of his mouth. The small amount of saliva disappeared like water into sand, but he was able to talk without each word ripping his throat. "I wish to God I could make up some story about working for the KGB, because that's all you seem to want to hear. But I can't; I just don't know that much about today's KGB. If I tried making up something, you'd know for sure I was lying, and I'd be in even worse shape than I am now, if that's possible. I haven't done any intelligence work since the early seventies."

Veil held his breath, half expecting to hear Parker walking away. But Parker stayed where he was.

"Tell me about your experiences with intelligence," the Army officer said quietly.

"I worked for the CIA."

"Wrong," Parker said disdainfully. "We've checked you out."

"My records have been doctored."

"I know that. The fact of the matter is that you were a turncoat. You went over. There's still some mystery as to how you got off so easily, and who was protecting you. I'm sure you'll clear up that little mystery for me during the course of this conversation. Like now."

"What you think I was or did isn't the point, Park—" Veil swallowed again, but he had no saliva left. His throat felt as if it were swelling shut, and he dropped his voice to a hoarse whisper. "What's important is that I *did* work for the Agency. They disapproved of something I did. I was put on a heavy shit list under sentence of being executed at some time in the indefinite future. End of story—except that's the reason I had to come back to the Institute after I'd killed your man."

"Then you *admit* that you killed him?"

"For Christ's sake, Parker. You know I did."

"Don't be a smart-ass, Kendry. If I remember correctly, you claimed at the time that it was a freak accident. I just wanted to set the record straight. You're the one who's going to die if I don't get the right answers, not me. So just answer my questions. Why come back after it looked like you were home free?"

"I need water," Veil said in a barely audible whisper. "Can't . . . talk."

Parker thought about it, then filled the ladle from a bucket at his feet and passed it down through the bars. Veil had to suppress tremors in his throat as he drank.

"More," Veil whispered. "Please."

"Earn it. What were you after?"

"Information; reasons. At first I thought the man might be a CIA agent sent to carry out my sentence. Then I realized it didn't make sense for the Agency to pick tight quarters like the Institute to kill me when they had all the time in the world and all of New York City to work in. It meant he was a double—"

"Bullshit."

"—sent by his controller to kill me. Somebody who knew my background made me and assumed—mistakenly—that I was here on assignment to flush out their organization. You've got guys with black hats in here, Parker. You've been infiltrated."

"I'm really sorry I gave you that water, jerk," Parker said with genuine disgust. "You're not as thirsty as I thought you were. It's a mistake I won't repeat. You really are a glutton for punishment."

"What I'm telling you is the truth," Veil said quickly, as Parker started to walk away. "It has to be. I came back to look for proof. Why is my story so goddam difficult for you to even consider?"

Parker suddenly wheeled and kicked savagely at the bars beside Veil's head. "Because we have *proof* that you're a Russian agent, jerk!" he shouted with unexpected and explosive rage. "They recruited you after you were booted out of the Army. You think I'm crazy? You think I'd make any man suffer what you're suffering without absolute proof that he was a dangerous enemy with secrets that threaten the security of my country? Your buddies are the barbarians, Kendry, not us. What you're going through is the kind of shit the KGB puts some of our people through, so we're just returning the favor. It's too bad you probably won't be alive to go back and tell them how much it hurts."

"Parker, you dumb son of a bitch, listen—"

"You're an idiot, because you think I'm going to eventually back off. You're wrong, buddy. You're going to go right on suffering until you die, or until I get the information I want. I want to know what network you're a part of, the name of your controller, and what specific information you were asked to gather. That's for openers. Later we'll get into more general discussions of KGB operations. You see, Kendry, you really have been wasting my time and your water by trying to bullshit me."

Veil closed his eyes for a few moments and again tried to focus his thoughts, this time on the question of whom Parker could have talked to. He was afraid he knew the answer; his unknown enemy had found a way to kill him without even coming near the cage or firing a bullet. "What proof?" he asked quietly.

"Never mind," Parker answered in a somewhat defensive tone. "I've got it."

"Who told you I was KGB?"

"How did you find the tunnel?"

"I just found it. I'd been looking for a way to get in here, and I got lucky."

"Where have you been hiding since you killed the Mamba?"

"At the hospice."

"How'd you get up there?"

"Pilgrim arranged it. He wants to know what's going on almost as much as I do."

"Why didn't he come to me?"

"You'll have to ask him."

"I'm asking you, jerk."

"I need water, Parker. I'm losing my voice."

"No way. You haven't paid for what I gave you before."

"I don't know why Pilgrim didn't want to talk to you."

"Take a guess."

"You know him better than I do, so you must know that he sometimes has funny reasons for doing things. I used to think that I understood his reasons. Now I'm not so sure."

"Does he know you're over here?"

"He'll probably guess, but I didn't tell him I was going."

"Why not?"

"I'm not sure I trust him any longer."

"Why."

"Personality conflict."

"Well, he can guess all he wants to," Parker said in a low,

ominous tone. "By the time I let him in here again, you'll either be dead and buried in the riverbank, or on your way to Washington for some really serious interrogation about your bosses and your network. Your choice."

"Damn it, Parker, I don't have even one boss, much less a network." Suddenly Veil found himself laughing—a high-pitched, tortured, hiccupping sound that would have sounded more like laughter if he weren't dying of thirst and exposure. "You know, man, you're unbelievably dense, and you're really starting to piss me off. Somebody's pulling your pud, and you're determined to kill off the one man who could help you find out who it is."

"Pilgrim's a fool," Parker said, more to himself than to Veil. "He'd give away the whole candy store."

"You're the one with the sucker in the shop, Colonel—not Pilgrim. *Think*, for chrissake! Did *you* send that Mamba after me?"

Parker's silence was eloquent.

"Of course not," Veil continued. "Do you know who did?"

Again, Parker's silence was his answer.

"Now we're getting somewhere," Veil said with a sigh, struggling for breath and against the impulse to gag. Each sound he made now translated itself into pain, but he had to keep talking, had to somehow make Parker listen and understand. "I'll bet you don't even know how your man got up on that mountain; I certainly don't, and neither does Pilgrim. But you *do* know that he went there and that he was after me. Why—if not for the reasons I'm giving you? He was a double agent, sent by his controller to kill me because the controller thought I was after him. Whoever fed you that shit about me being KGB could be the man I'm after."

"It doesn't have to be that way," Parker said tightly.

"What doesn't have to be what way?"

"Your scenario of what happened."

"Fine. Tell me what the Mamba was doing on Pilgrim's mountain. Do you think he got lost during a training exercise and stopped by the pool to ask me directions?"

"He was a double agent, all right, but he was *your* man."

"*My* man?" Veil coughed and tasted blood as his lower lip split in two places.

"You were his controller."

"Come on, Parker. Appearances to the contrary, it can't be *that* easy to seed an agent into your operation here. Once having done so, why should I kill him?"

"That's one of the things you're going to tell me right now, Kendry. And if you don't, you've had your last drop of water in this lifetime."

"You're crazy, Parker. How in hell could I be that joker's controller? I've been living in New York for more than fifteen years."

"Right. The question is what you've been doing in New York."

"I thought you said you'd checked up on me. I'm a painter; I've been painting, stupid."

"What else? What did the Russians have you doing in New York? And why should they assign this Mamba to you?"

Veil choked off a curse and shook his head in frustration. Arguing with Parker was futile, and the fever in his mind and body told him that it was long past time for him to roll out the heavy artillery. "Parker, you fucking idiot, I want you to call a man by the name of Orville Madison. CIA. I don't have the slightest idea where he's posted now, but Langley will have the information. He was my controller. You're DIA, and you should have enough juice to get the Agency to cooperate with you. Madison hates my guts, but I don't think he'll lie to you—assuming he'll talk to you in the first place. Madison will give you the straight story on me, right up to the minute I arrived at the Institute."

"How would he know?"

"Because he's had me flagged from the day I was thrown out of the Army and the CIA. I have no doubt that he's bugged every place I've lived in and knows the birthmarks of every person I've met with since then. Madison can probably tell you what I had for breakfast some Sunday morning ten years ago. He'll tell you I'm not KGB. The same person who sent the Mamba after me is trying to kill me now in a different way, by framing me and getting you to kill me."

"Orville Madison, huh?" For the first time, Parker seemed interested in what Veil had to say.

"If you can't get to Madison right away, try getting in touch with a man by the name of Lester Bean. Bean may be easier to trace, if you go right to your boss in the Pentagon. Bean was a colonel, and my CO in Vietnam."

Veil waited, but there was no immediate response from Parker. "Orville Madison—CIA," Veil repeated. "Lester Bean, at one time an officer in the U.S. Army. Call them, Parker. Learn the truth. And then please bring me some water, because I'm really not feeling too well."

And then Veil passed out.

Chapter 20

Veil dreams.

Spring. The Greenwich Village Art Show. Surrounded by his oil paintings, he sits in a tattered canvas folding chair on Christopher Street.

He is terribly thirsty; he is so thirsty that he cannot focus on the potential customers who walk by or occasionally stop to look at his work. Everything seems to be covered with pink gauze, as in fever-vision. He has a pounding headache, and he can think of nothing but water. He is near a number of bars, and he knows where there is a fountain, but he does not bother to rise and go to look for water, for he knows there will be none. Veil knows he is dreaming, and around his dream is a steel cage.

"You're a dead man, Kendry."

Veil squints through the haze at Madison, who is emerging

143

from a taxicab. The CIA controller's shoes are covered with steaming, green jungle mud.

The dream is out of control, Veil thinks, with disparate times, places, people, and things all bleeding into one another. He is dying, and he is both afraid and enraged. He could roll out of the dream, but chooses not to; a waking state will bring him only the worse torment of the cage and the sun.

"Tell Parker the truth, Madison," Veil says to the man at the curb with the rotting jungle mud on his shoes. "Kill me with a bullet, a knife, or a garrote—not a lie."

Footsteps come up behind him, and Parker's voice whispers in his ear. "He can guess all he wants to. By the time I let him in here again, you'll either be dead and buried in the riverbank or—"

Veil wheels, causing the pink fever-haze to swirl around him, but Parker is gone.

"I really wish I could get the two of you together," Veil says, and begins to laugh hysterically.

"He can guess all he wants to," Parker intones from the bottom of a well.

"Madison, don't kill me with a lie!"

"You're a dead man, Kendry. I'm going to shoot your ass on the day you find peace or happiness."

"Orville, old stick!" Veil shouts. "Today isn't that day! I'm really not very happy, so don't let this stupid bastard kill me!"

I'm losing it, Veil thinks as he suddenly finds himself standing in the middle of Christopher Street with cars passing through him. Thirst, exposure, exhaustion and fear are taking their toll, ripping up his mind.

There is no place left to escape to.

"Tell him the truth, Madison. You execute me as you see fit, but please get me out of this cage. I don't want to die like an animal. I don't deserve this."

Raskolnikov, the White Russian art dealer who will become Veil's mentor, rounds a corner. The portly, bearded man carries an ivory-handled cane in one hand and a chocolate ice-cream cone in the other. His black patent-leather shoes flash in the sunlight; his footsteps explode on the sidewalk like beats of a snare drum.

Madison, Po, Sharon, Parker, Pilgrim, and Perry Tompkins are all in the crowd.

I am dying.

Raskolnikov glances at Veil's paintings and walks on. He crosses the street at the intersection, steps up on the curb, and stops. He stands still for some time, absently licking his ice-cream cone as people pass by on either side of him. Then he abruptly tosses his cone into a wire trash container, wheels around, and comes back across the intersection against the light. A car screeches to a halt, narrowly missing him, but Raskolnikov does not even seem to notice.

"Dead and buried in the riverbank," Parker whispers in Veil's ear.

Raskolnikov again walks past Veil's paintings, but immediately turns, comes back, and stops in front of them.

"Call Madison or Bean," Veil whispers. "Please, please. Please. I'm so thirsty."

"Interesting," Raskolnikov says as he turns toward Veil. "One really has to view your paintings out of the corner of the eye."

Chapter 21

The cold water splashed over his fever-hot body like a tidal wave of torment. Veil's muscles knotted and quivered, but he only had enough strength to lick the water off his cracked lips. He allowed himself to fall sideways, and he sucked at the wet ground. He kept glancing to the side, waiting—praying—for the ladle of water to be offered through the bars. It did not come.

"Please give me water," Veil said. Or thought he said. He would do anything now for water—beg, make up a story about the Russians and the KGB; but he could not even be sure that he was speaking loud or clear enough to be understood.

Parker's voice was strangely hollow, as if the man were speaking to him from the opposite end of a large cavern. "You've got balls, Kendry. I'll say that for you. You really are going to manage to kill yourself. Do you think we're idiots?"

Veil somehow managed to rise to his knees. He clutched at the bars, resting his head against the steel. "Don't . . . understand. Give me water. You've got what you wanted."

"You're crazy," Parker replied in a tone in which outrage, confusion, and genuine distress vied for control. "You think I want to watch a crazy man kill himself? What the hell did you think you were doing? Did you think you could bluff me? How can a man be dying of *thirst*, for chrissake, and still find the will to lie?"

"Don't understand. Call Madison. CIA."

"The CIA's never heard of you or anyone named Orville Madison."

"No. Not true. Lie. You didn't talk to the right people, or . . . Madison told them to lie. Call Bean."

"Bean retired six years ago, and he was killed in an automobile accident three months later. You probably knew that."

"No. Madison . . ."

"There is no Orville Madison. You pulled the name out of a very dry hat."

Something was wrong, Veil thought as he struggled to hide from the agony in his mind and body in order to concentrate. There was something in Parker's tone, something in the dream, that told him what was wrong, but he could not pull his thoughts together, could not make the connection. "No," he whispered, feeling lost. "Madison was my controller. Not his style to . . . let this happen. Who did you talk to?"

There was a long pause. Veil moved his head slightly in order to look up at Parker, but he could see only a blurred image.

"You're going to die, Kendry," Parker said in a husky voice filled with emotion. "I wouldn't have believed any man could do to himself what you're doing. I wish I could say that I admire your guts, but I don't. You're just stupid. I don't want you to die. Do you understand? I really don't. But I can't let you screw us, either. Don't you understand that I *know* you're KGB? Kendry, I *know* you're lying. One thing; just give me one thing and I take you out. Give me the name of your controller."

"Madison. CIA."

"Stop it! You're finished, Kendry! No man can endure more than you've endured. Let it go. If I take you out now, give you some water and medical attention, you'll be all right. Another few hours and you'll be finished. Stop telling me lies and give me the name of your Russian controller. It won't take me long to check. I may even give you a long drink right now."

"You didn't talk to anyone."

"The name of your controller, Kendry! What specific information did you hope to get here? Give me *something*, will you? I want to take you out. I don't want to see you die for nothing!"

"Not you. You didn't make the calls personally. Someone else. Who?"

"Damn you, Kendry!" Parker shouted. "Damn your eyes! If you think the communists are going to take over the world because you're tougher than we are, you've got a big surprise coming! Fuck you! Die!"

Veil waited a few moments, then looked up again and squinted. The blurred image was gone. He groaned and licked at the moisture left on the bars of his cage.

Chapter 22

Veil dreams.

Out of control in mind and body, he speeds down the endless corridor between the swirling gray walls in which figures move and occasionally beckon. He does not try to roll out of the dream, or even slow himself, for there is less agony here.

There is no agony here.

In the corridor, speeding toward the electric-blue horizon, there is no thirst or fever-heat or pain. He will not go back, he thinks. Never. He will suffer no more. He will fly along this corridor until he dies, if he is not dead already.

We're looking for heaven.

Familiar, disembodied voices call out from the mist on either side of him.

"He can guess all he wants to. By the time I let him in here again, you'll either be dead and buried in the riverbank or on

151

your way to Washington for more detailed interrogation about your bosses and your network."

"Ah, but you blew it, dummy," Veil replies in a casual tone that issues from his chest, throat, and mouth as a series of soft chiming notes. "If you're still interested in the truth, give my buddy Orville a little ding-a-ling. But *you* call him. Don't let anyone else do it for you."

"You're a dead man, Kendry. I'm going to shoot your ass on the day when you're happy."

For a few moments, Veil considers remaining silent; he no longer cares about anything but remaining in the state he is in.

"Good luck, Orville," Veil says at last. "I *am* at peace here, and I am happy; and there isn't a damn thing you can do about it. Even you can't reach into heaven. Shoot away."

Chimes suddenly sound. They are outside himself, very loud, and reverberate in the corridor.

"Madison! Tell Parker the truth! Kill me with a bullet, not a lie!"

He does care.

His speed increases. If he is not dead, Veil thinks, he is certainly now very close to it. He is sorry he has never found the courage to look directly into the walls. He would look now, but he is going too fast; he is at once paralyzed and elongated; he feels as if his body is stretched out for miles behind him, and he cannot turn his head.

"Stop it! Kendry, I don't want you to die!"

Chimes. *Bong*! *Bong*! *Bong*!

"Parker! Hey, dummy, pick up the phone and make the call! Call Madison!"

His speed increases even more. The moaning, chiming walls flash past in a blur. Veil feels as if his body is coming apart, stretched so thin that there is nothing left but spinning atoms that somehow still carry the electrical charges of emotion and thought.

Then, suddenly, pain pierces heaven.

Something sharp, like a snake's fangs, sink into the floating atoms where his right shoulder had been. He wants to grab the wound, but he is stretched too thin. He cannot find his hand.

"Interesting," Raskolnikov says. "One really has to view your paintings out of the corner of the eye."

"He can guess all he wants to."

"You're a dead man, Kendry."

"*Sharon! I love you!*"

"By the time I let him in here again—"

"*Sharon, I'm sorry we didn't have time!*"

We're looking for heaven.

Venom spurts into the wound, into and around the atoms. There is more pain. His atoms sting, swell, and throb. He can feel the venom, as hot and corrosive as acid, searing his atoms as it moves, seeps through the spaces where his limbs used to be. It is soaking into his space-body, inexorably heading for his brain. His atoms suddenly begin to vibrate in unison, producing low, booming chime sounds that steadily rise in pitch and volume until at last they are beyond hearing.

Then the venom fills his skull, soaking his brain, and he explodes soundlessly in a cloud of electric blue.

Chapter 23

He erupted through a veil of electric blue consciousness
to find himself lying on the ground on his back staring up at
the night sky through lines of steel that were the bars forming
the roof of his cage. His entire body was clenched in a seizure
that was virtually epileptic; his hands flopped back and forth
in front of his face and occasionally shot out to bang against
the bars on either side of him; his knees knocked together, and
the back of his head beat a syncopated tattoo against the
ground. However, even in the midst of the neurological storm
that was raging through his body, Veil noticed that his vision
and thoughts seemed remarkably clear. It was as though he
had somehow been anesthetized against the physical and
mental agony he had been experiencing. He was still thirsty
beyond any degree he could have previously imagined, but
this need for water no longer crowded everything else out of

his mind; he felt like some flesh-and-blood tuning fork vibrating, aglow, with raw energy and ready to fly apart.

And his right shoulder still hurt.

The needle pain he had felt had been just that, Veil thought—a needle. Somebody had given him a hot shot of a drug powerful enough to make him feel as if he could literally burst out of his cage, even as he flayed his skin and broke his bones in the process.

Then the seizure passed. Veil lay still for a few moments, sucking the cool night air into his wracked, dry lungs and staring at the stars. Finally he let his right hand drop to his side, and his fingers touched something soft. He rolled over in the cramped space and got up on his knees. Beside him were a large canteen, a neatly folded jumpsuit dyed in a camouflage pattern, and a leather pouch fastened at the top with a drawstring that was a thin leather thong.

The door to his cage was propped open with a stick.

With shaking hands, Veil struggled frantically to unscrew the top of the canteen. He finally managed to get the cap off, then straightened up so fast that he banged his head on the bars above him. He rolled over on his left side, lifted the canteen, and let the cool water pour into his mouth and splash over his face. Although he knew better, he swallowed the water in great, heaving gulps, and could not stop until his belly was painfully bloated and he vomited. There was plenty of water left, though, and he forced himself to wait for a minute or two, then lifted the canteen to his lips and drank more sparingly. When he felt his belly beginning to swell, he took the canteen away from his mouth. He shook it to reassure himself that there was still water left, then—despite the conviction that he could drink water steadily for a week without being sated—screwed the cap back on. The drug—which Veil assumed was some kind of super-amphetamine and which had probably been developed at the Army complex—and the water had carried him past his most immediate physical crisis.

He considered the possibility that Parker's gut abhorrence of torture had finally gotten the best of the colonel, and the stimulant, clothes, and water were merely Parker's invitation to him to go out into the night to be shot by some Mamba with a Sniperscope. He decided that it was unlikely; if Parker had wanted to back down from his challenge to Veil's life, there would then be no sense in killing him. There were other means of interrogation, principally chemical. In any case, Veil thought, the question of who was responsible for his sudden deliverance, and why it was being offered, was resoundingly irrelevant. He was definitely not going to hang around any longer to brood over it. He picked up the clothes, pouch, and canteen, and crawled through the narrow steel aperture to freedom.

Feeling as if he would take off and fly away if he did not concentrate on staying grounded, Veil ran low and hard through the moon-shadows cast by the surrounding mountains, streaking across the dirt practice field used by the Mambas to the riverbank. He set the articles he was carrying down in the tall, thick grass, then rolled down the steep incline of the bank into the river. This time he was prepared for the gelid punch of the water, and the agony of sudden, icy cold branding burned flesh was bittersweet; it hurt in every fiber of his being, but the torment was also a ringing affirmation that he was still alive, and free.

He could also drink all of this water he wanted to—something he proceeded to do while he anchored himself against the swift-moving current by grabbing hold of naked roots that jutted from the dirt bank.

Still not completely sated but comfortable, Veil pulled himself out of the water and crawled up the bank. He dried himself off with clumps of grass, then dressed in the jumpsuit, which proved to be lightweight but warm. He felt light-headed now but still bursting with energy which he knew was false, artificially induced by the powerful drug. Already he had begun to think ahead, trying to plan; he knew he must eventually "crash" as the price to be paid for this energy, and possibly crash very hard. He had to find a safe place to land.

Kneeling on the ground, he loosened the top of the leather pouch and spilled its contents out on the grass. There were at least two dozen sinewy strips of beef jerky coated with a flexible, transparent gel that Veil assumed was a high-concentrate protein and vitamin supplement. There was a tube of an antibiotic, anesthetic skin cream; several packets of coarse-textured brown tablets that were unlabeled and individually wrapped in cellophane; and his .38—loaded.

He stripped off the jumpsuit, smeared salve from the tube on his burned face and body. The sunburn pain began to go away almost immediately as the cream dissolved into his skin. He dressed again, put his revolver in a shoulder pocket of the jumpsuit, then replaced the other items in the bag and drew the drawstring tight. After refilling his canteen he began walking inland, keeping low in the tall grass along the riverbank. Although he knew he was leaving a trail that could be easily followed by almost anyone, his most immediate concern was the danger of being spotted through a Sniper-scope or infrared binoculars; it would certainly not be long before he was missed.

He had an ally in the camp, Veil thought—perhaps. He would take nothing for granted any longer in this strange place, these mountains and this valley, haunted by one man's bizarre obsession. Since, to Parker, it was evident that Veil would die before he told the "truth," it had occurred to Veil that the officer had decided to use him as fodder in a Mamba training exercise.

But a loaded .38 made him rather dangerous fodder. Mambas might be able to snatch many things out of the air, but they didn't catch bullets.

Whatever the reason for his freedom, Veil thought, the fact of the matter was that he was free. Now he had to decide what to do with that freedom. He had no idea of how far the compound extended inland, and his only purpose now was to put as much distance as possible between himself and the main installation while he waited to see what the side effects of the drug would be. Then he would have to avoid capture while he tried to figure out a way of getting back to the main Institute complex, assuming that was what he wanted to do, and he was not at all certain that it was. Somehow managing to get out of the Army compound and back to the hospice or Institute was an escape, but not a solution. He would be left back where he had started. After his thirsty conversations with Parker, Veil was convinced that the Army compound was where the answers to his questions lay. The trick was not to die from an overdose of action.

He assumed that the Mambas were more than deadly fighting machines; they would be trained to track, and track very well. So far, he'd left behind him what amounted to an eight-lane highway; now it was time to mine that highway with a bit of consternation and confusion.

He stopped dead in his tracks, then stripped off his jumpsuit and rolled the pouch and canteen in it. Then he began walking backwards along his own trail. After he had retreated twenty yards he hopped sideways onto a rock, and from this perch dove down the incline of the riverbank. He rolled into the water and, holding his bundle above his head, let the current carry him another forty yards downstream before he grabbed a root and hauled himself ashore on an area that was an extended rock shelf. He dressed "wet" so as not to disturb the surrounding grass, smeared his face and hair with mud, then walked up the rock shelf, which extended up and over the bank.

Suddenly he began to tremble violently, and almost lost his balance. His vision blurred and the muscles in his stomach knotted, doubling him over with pain.

Drug reaction.

Veil sat down hard on the stone. Grimacing against the pain of the cramps in his stomach, he fumbled with the drawstring on the leather pouch. He opened the pouch, reached in, and withdrew one of the packets of brown pills. Without hesitation, he put one in his mouth and washed it down with a swallow of water from his canteen. Within moments he was better, and in less than five minutes the muscle spasms had completely vanished and his vision cleared.

Although he was not hungry, he forced himself to eat one of the strips of beef jerky—and found it so good that he promptly ate two more. Then he rose and, keeping to stone and hard-packed gravel whenever possible, started across the width of the valley.

Dawn found him on the opposite side of the valley, resting in a thick copse of trees. And thinking.

Veil was in superb condition. He continued to rest throughout the morning, sipping water and eating the fortified beef jerky. He still had attacks of cramps and blurred vision, but the spells became steadily less severe, less frequent, and were of shorter duration. He knew that it would take days, perhaps weeks, for his body to fully recover from his two-day ordeal, but by mid-afternoon he felt strong enough to put the plan he had formulated into action. He would have preferred to stay in hiding for at least another day to free himself even more from dependency on the drug and its debilitating side effects, but he had begun to experience a strong sense of urgency. The fact that he had escaped with the aid of a secret ally in the compound had to be making his enemy extremely nervous, and Veil wanted to give the man as little time to plan and act— or escape—as possible.

Veil emptied the leather pouch. He put a few of the pills in the pocket with his gun, then proceeded, with the aid of a sharp rock, to separate the patches of leather that made up the pouch along their seams. These he knotted together into a single strap that was almost a yard long. At one end of the strap he tied the drawstring. Then, moving very slowly and carefully, he again started inland.

A half hour later he found the precise terrain he had been looking for. He took a few sips of water and threw the canteen away; he would not be needing it any longer. Then he began moving toward the center of the valley, purposely leaving a subtle but nonetheless visible trail that he knew could be followed by a skilled tracker. He went ten yards past a tree with thick foliage and low-hanging branches, then stopped and carefully back-tracked to the tree. He took one of the pills as a precautionary measure, then swung up into the branches of the tree, squatted down in the *V* between a limb and the trunk, and waited.

He had anticipated advanced tracking skills, cunning, and stealth in the Mambas, had, in fact, been counting on these skills and was on constant alert; still, he almost missed the Mamba who had picked up his trail. The man, expertly camouflaged, was only fifteen yards away when Veil spotted a slight movement in the tall grass and a flash of metallic gray that would be a machine pistol.

Then the man froze; from the angle of the Mamba's camouflaged cap, Veil could tell that he was studying the tree. Veil remained perfectly still in his position on the opposite side of the trunk. After a minute or two, the Mamba began moving again.

Veil dropped soundlessly to the ground, then stood with his back to the trunk and his .38 held up next to his right ear. He counted slowly to twenty, then spun out into the center of the trail he had made and aimed his pistol at the spot where he judged the Mamba's forehead should be.

His timing was virtually flawless. He found himself standing directly in front of the green-eyed, pock-faced Mamba who had studied him so intently in the commons area; the barrel of Veil's gun was no more than three inches from the Mamba's forehead. The man instantly froze and gave a little grunt that was half fear, half disgust.

"That's good," Veil said in a flat voice. "Stay that way."

"Fuck you," the Mamba replied evenly. But he did not move.

"We're on the same side, pal."

"You say."

"I don't want to even hear you fart, much less move the wrong way. I don't want to kill an American serviceman, but I will if I have to."

"You've already killed one. Dan Gurran was a friend of mine."

"Well, dear old Dan was trying his damndest to kill me, and I assure you that he wasn't a friend of yours. No matter. I'd like to point out that I haven't killed you—yet. That seems a strong argument for my good intentions."

"Don't try to bullshit me, Kendry. Whether you kill me or not, you still won't be able to get out of here. You probably think I'm more valuable to you alive than dead. You're wrong. You can't use me as a hostage. You think this is a Boy Scout camp?"

"Very carefully, now: Flip that weapon in the air, grab it by the barrel and hold it out to me. If I don't like the way you do it, I'll splatter your brains and soothe my conscience by reminding myself that you're not a Boy Scout."

The Mamba, eyes fixed on Veil's gun, did as he was told. Veil took the machine pistol in his left hand and broke open the magazine against his left thigh. He flung the pistol in one direction, the magazine in another.

"Now your knife," Veil said curtly.

The man shook his head. "I don't have one."

Veil made the man remove his boots and pull up his pant legs; there was no ankle scabbard. When the man pulled up his jacket and shirt, nothing showed but bare midriff.

"Lie down on your belly," Veil commanded. "Arms and legs spread-eagled."

Again the Mamba obeyed. Veil knelt down on one knee between the man's outstretched legs and pressed the barrel of his revolver against the base of the man's spine. He knew that for a man like this Mamba, the thought of ending up paralyzed and in a wheelchair for the rest of his life would be more frightening than death.

"You and I are going to have a little chat, my friend," Veil continued easily.

"If the price of my life or legs is information, you may as well start shooting right now," the Mamba said in a voice that was thin but steady. "I'm not going to tell you anything."

"Wait until you hear what I have to say. We—and I'm talking about two Americans, as well as two human beings— have a problem here. I think you're really going to want to help me solve it."

"You're the one with the problem, Kendry. No matter what you do to me, you're not getting out of this valley alive."

"Listen to me," Veil said in a low voice as he increased the pressure of his gun against the man's spine. "You've got an enemy agent here—and a top-ranking one. He's probably working for the Russians, but I can't be sure."

"You're full of shit, Kendry. You're the enemy agent. And it makes me sick to my stomach to hear you call yourself an American. You're a traitor."

"Who's really in charge of this place?"

The Mamba moved his head slightly. Veil pressed gun against bone sharply, and the man stiffened. "Easy," the Mamba whispered. "I haven't tried anything."

"Don't. Answer my question. It's harmless enough; as you say, I'm not going anywhere."

"It's a stupid question, because you know the answer."

"I've got a flash for you, pal. I think Parker's number two around here. Think about it. Have you ever had any indication that Parker takes orders from someone else? I mean, someone here, someone who may not be in uniform."

"Fuck you, traitor. You're either out of your mind or fishing for something else; either way, I'm not going to answer any more questions."

"Get up," Veil said, rising to his feet and backing away slightly. "Put your hands in the air and turn around slowly."

"Are you going to kill me?" the Mamba asked in a neutral tone as he rose and turned.

"I don't think so; not as long as you continue to behave yourself."

The man's eyes narrowed. "I can't believe that you took out Dan in a fair fight, Kendry. I really wish I could get a shot at you myself."

"Not today, pal," Veil replied laconically. "I doubt that I'd be much of a match for a big, young bull like you. My guest accommodations here left a little to be desired, as you may have noticed. I'm still a little shaky. Besides, I'm pushing forty. Why would you want to beat up on an old man?" Veil paused, smiled thinly, then tossed his revolver to the Mamba. "Merry Christmas."

The startled Mamba snatched the .38 out of the air, immediately stepped forward, and pressed the bore squarely against Veil's forehead. His green eyes gleamed. "Want to test my reflexes, Kendry?"

"No."

"What the hell do you think you're doing? You just signed your own death warrant."

"I sincerely hope not. I'm feeling generous, and I gave you my gun as a gesture of goodwill. Now I'm your prisoner. Take me to your leader."

"Are you trying to be funny?"

Veil sighed. "I want you to take me to Parker, pal—with as little fuss and as quickly as you can, if you don't mind. I'd just as soon nobody saw us."

"Parker's dead."

Veil felt a sudden, sharp pain in his stomach that had nothing to do with the drug he had been taking. His enemy was in an even bigger hurry than he'd thought, and his own plan was rapidly falling apart. "Shit," he said quietly. "When?"

"A half hour after you escaped. You should know; you killed him."

"Smell the barrel of that gun. It hasn't been fired in the past twenty-four hours."

"You killed Colonel Parker with his own gun. And what the fuck am I doing standing here talking to you? Turn around and start walking, Kendry. Hands clasped behind your head."

Veil remained still, chafing at the knowledge that he'd lost a day. "Why would I give you my gun if I'd killed Parker?"

"Because you're a smart-ass who isn't half as clever as he thinks he is. Once you got out of the cage and killed the Colonel, you realized that you couldn't get out of the compound on your own. Maybe you thought you'd bluff your way out."

"You do have to get me out," Veil said evenly, fighting against the panic he felt welling in him. There was just no way to rush what he had to do. "And you have to do it quickly. Every minute we stand here means that other lives are in danger. It also means that the man you really want is probably putting more distance between us."

"You must take me for a fool."

Veil took three quick steps backward; at each step the firing pin of his .38 fell on an empty chamber. The Mamba cursed and threw the revolver away.

"I mentioned that I was feeling generous," Veil said as he took the knotted strap he had made from the leather pouch and drawstring out of his breast pocket. "I didn't say suicidal."

The Mamba instantly went into a fighting stance, forming the fingers of his left hand into a claw that was thrust out at eye level. The right hand flicked to a hidden scabbard behind his neck and came away gripping a large Bowie knife. Then he began to move, circling Veil, varying his speed, knife hand and empty hand weaving intricate, hypnotic patterns in the air less than two feet from Veil's face.

Veil, who had spent ten years learning classic *kata* and another ten unlearning them, knew pretty much what to expect from the other man. He leaned back slightly from the darting blade but remained relaxed, the leather strap dangling from his right hand. He fixed his gaze on the Mamba's waist and hips, forecasters of movement, and allowed his peripheral vision to track the swirling movement of the knife; any sudden lunge or extension of the knife hand would be signaled a fraction of a second beforehand by a movement of the hips.

First came a feint with the knife, which Veil ignored, then a sidekick, which was parried. He did not try to counterpunch or kick; the knife in the Mamba's hand was too dangerous for that, allowing no margin of error.

Veil had no doubt that the Mamba's master was well versed in many schools of combat, but the Mamba was simply too young to have gone much beyond becoming master of one style, which in this case was Japanese. The Mamba was most likely unfamiliar with Thai "scarf" fighting, with which a master could successfully defend himself against an armed attacker, in the meantime blinding or strangling his opponent, using no more than a simple handkerchief which he had wetted with his own saliva. And a whip, Veil thought, was considerably more deadly than a handkerchief.

165

A slight cocking of the Mamba's hips indicated to Veil that the man was getting ready for a combination of side and roundhouse kicks, which would probably be followed by a figure-eight attack with the knife hand. A split second before the first kick could be thrown, Veil flicked his right wrist. The leather strap darted through the air, and the drawstring tip snapped at the end with the speed of sound, producing a sharp crack. The Mamba arched his back an instant too late, and fear for his eyes flashed across the muscles of his face. Slowly blood began to fill a three-inch welt on his right cheekbone.

Veil's strike had caused the other man to lose his concentration and rhythm, and he reflexively reached up to touch the cut on his cheek. In that moment he was vulnerable, but still Veil waited.

As the Mamba recovered and again started to assume a fighting stance, Veil flicked his improvised whip twice—once at the groin and once at the knife hand. The second strike hit across the back of the man's hand, drawing blood. The Mamba ignored the pain and instantly lunged forward with his knife, but Veil was ready. He leapt to one side and spun away, at the same time flicking the whip at the man's eyes. The Mamba backed away. His tongue darted out, licked his lips.

Now the Mamba began to take defensive maneuvers against Veil's whip, slashing across his body at the flying leather. The focus of his attention shifted from Veil to the whip popping in front of him, and it was the mistake Veil had been waiting for. He purposely snapped the whip wide, beside the Mamba's left ear. Instantly Veil spun clockwise, knowing that he had only microseconds to act. Even as the man was slashing across his body, Veil's heel was inexorably moving toward the exposed right side of the man's rib cage. The blow landed, breaking two ribs. Veil kept moving, spinning out of the way as the Mamba, showing an incredible tolerance for pain, spun and slashed back through the space where Veil's belly had been only an instant before. But now Veil was behind him. Veil looped the strap around the man's neck, grabbed both ends, and pulled.

The Mamba, knowing that a single, sharp pull would kill him, panicked; he dropped the knife and clutched at the strap around his neck with both hands. Veil released the strap and drove a fist into the man's broken ribs. The man screamed in agony and dropped to his knees. Veil darted around to the front, his fist raised for another blow. But the Mamba was finished, his glazed green eyes clearly reflecting defeat by the pain in his body and fear of Veil's overwhelming mastery of the martial arts.

"Now I hope you'll listen to me," Veil said, cupping the man's chin with his right hand and lifting his head. "Parker didn't, and it cost him his life. I am not a fucking agent for anyone; I'm a painter. If I don't get out of here alive, you remember this conversation—but don't repeat it to anyone here in the compound. Wait until the investigators come in. If I'm killed, it's going to be up to you to clean house—or see that someone else cleans it. You may not know who Parker's superior is around here, but the Pentagon certainly does. There may be other doubles, so watch your ass. I'm sorry I had to bust you up, but you didn't give me a whole hell of a lot of choice. If you're ever in New York, look me up; I owe you a drink."

Then Veil knocked the man unconscious with a simple, hard right cross.

Chapter 24

Veil, his long hair tied up beneath the Mamba's camouflage cap with his leather strap, began making his way back across the width of the valley, heading for the river. He chafed at the slowness of his pace, but knew that he could not go faster without risking detection; he had to mimic the tracking maneuvers of the Mambas and hope that he was not identified by someone on high ground with powerful binoculars.

He paused to eat the last of the beef jerky; he forced himself to eat all of it; he would now need all of his dwindling reserves of energy for an unknown period of time. Although he was still free of symptoms, and even though he knew he could be risking convulsions from an overdose, he took three of the brown pills—as much for the strength they would give him as to prevent withdrawal symptoms. Then he went on.

The sound of soft chimes was with him constantly now. However, this music of peril was not clear and close behind his eyes, but muffled and welling from somewhere deep in his soul. The chimes were not for him.

Veil feared he was already too late.

It was dusk by the time he reached the riverbank, the rising moon obscured by clouds scudding across a dull copper sky. He walked upstream until he found what he was looking for—a log jammed between two boulders. Using the Mamba's machine pistol like a crowbar, Veil freed the log, then wrapped his arms around it from the side and let the log carry him out into the swift-moving current as he clasped the machine pistol between his knees.

If there were any Mambas tracking along the riverbank, Veil did not see them; more important, they did not see him, for in what seemed a very short time, he was closing on the brightly floodlit area that extended thirty yards beyond the concrete wall spanning the valley and marking the boundary of the Army compound. Peering over the top of the log, Veil could see two uniformed soldiers on top of the wall, each armed with a machine gun and scanning the river on both sides of the wall.

He was operating on three key assumptions, Veil thought as he sucked in a deep breath, released his grip on the log, and let the churning current carry him under. One, the Army was far more concerned with keeping intruders out than keeping them in; two, the fast flow of the river at the end of its journey to the sea was, in itself, a deterrent to covert movement upstream; therefore, three, the barrier extending below the surface—and there had to be one—would not be heavy-duty.

He would either be proved right, Veil thought, or disproved dead. There was no going back.

Gripping the machine pistol in his left hand, he pulled with his right and kicked, angling toward the bottom. He could see nothing in the icy darkness and had to rely on touch alone. Rested, relaxed, and after hyperventilation, Veil could hold his breath under water for almost two and a half minutes. In his present situation he guessed that he had close to two minutes before he would be forced to return to the surface—probably to be machine-gunned on sight. Or he could choose to drown, a notion he considered not without some irony in view of how desperately he had craved a drink only the day before. Except that this drink would kill him.

His fingers touched heavy netting, the most suitable choice for a barrier since it could be lowered to release heavy debris. Veil had the Mamba's Bowie knife but made an instant decision not to waste time and air trying to use it to cut through the netting, which would almost certainly be wire-reinforced and very difficult to cut through with anything but wire clippers. Instead he pulled himself along the bottom of the relatively shallow river until he touched what he had been hoping to find—a strip of concrete that served as a footing in which to anchor the net with wire grommets set in steel rings.

The pressure in his lungs was building.

With the current pressing him into the net, Veil planted his feet on the concrete on either side of the grommet. Using touch to guide him, he threaded the barrel of the machine pistol through the grommet. With the end of the barrel firmly set on the concrete, he grabbed the stock with both hands and exerted a steady, backward pull.

Nothing happened. The grommet held firm.

Veil relaxed his grip, then tried again, pushing with his legs and pulling with all his might, afraid that at any moment he would feel metal bend, or snap at a weld. After a few seconds he detected slight movement. He pushed the barrel through the grommet even further, then yanked with all his strength.

The grommet gave, and a ten-yard section of netting suddenly billowed downstream, carrying Veil with it.

Veil let go of the machine pistol, turned in the water, and pushed off the bottom, knifing upward at an angle that he hoped would bring him to the surface beyond the floodlit area on the other side of the wall.

He came up in cool night, near the bank. He half expected to hear shouts of alarm and warning, or automatic-weapons fire; but the only sounds that came to his ears were his own hoarse gasps and the rushing water. He sucked in air, rolled on his back, and let the current carry him downstream.

Exhausted, his mind and body drained by his continuing ordeal, Veil was almost swept down the channel that branched off from the waterfall and emptied into the sea. At the last moment Veil recognized the danger, rolled over, and knifed under water to reduce the drag of the water. He pulled, kicked, corkscrewed to his left, and surfaced in the somewhat calmer channel that ran past the waterfall. Gasping for breath, light-headed and knowing that he was dangerously close to losing consciousness, Veil dragged himself up on a rock shelf at the foot of the towering cliff he had dived off to begin his journey into the Army compound.

Above him was the hospice, and the steel cords supporting the cable car cut across the night sky to link the hospice to the main Institute complex on top of the mountain across the valley. Like an umbilical cord linking mother to child, Veil thought—except that in Jonathan Pilgrim's mind the hospice, a base camp for a desperate search, had always been the mother; the Institute was just an excuse for Pilgrim to probe the nature of the place where his soul had journeyed at the time of his death.

Veil sprawled out on the rock shelf and rested until his breathing became normal. Then he took a series of deep, measured breaths and tried to relax and marshal his energy. When he began to shiver with cold, he rose and ran in place in an attempt to generate body heat. He considered stripping off the wet jumpsuit, but decided that, even wet, the cotton provided needed insulation against the chill night air.

With the cold in him temporarily beaten back, Veil began moving along the face of the cliff, exploring its stone surface with his hands. The cliff appeared impossible to climb, yet one or more Mambas had periodically come through the mountain caves to penetrate and spy on the compound. Even Mambas didn't fly, and Veil was certain there had to be a relatively easy route up to the hospice.

He found it fifteen yards from the waterfall—steel pitons driven into crevices in the rock face. He grabbed the first piton and began to climb up the vertical wall.

Halfway up he suddenly began to tremble and cramp.

Unwilling to release the pitons with either hand to fumble for the pills, unsure of his remaining strength and equilibrium, Veil pressed his body against the rock face and waited. Fortunately, the spasms turned out to be relatively mild and passed quickly. Fighting dizziness, he completed the climb to the top.

He rested on the edge of the cliff for a half minute, then ran to Sharon Solow's office. He found Perry Tompkins absently swinging back and forth in the swivel chair before the computer terminal. The huge painter's head snapped around as Veil burst into the office, and his coal-black eyes glinted with excitement and pleasure.

"So?" Tompkins said, raising one eyebrow slightly. "Did you have a good time?"

Veil smiled thinly. "Not really. I don't think I'll go back, and I definitely will not recommend the place to my friends."

"Did you find what you were looking for?" Tompkins asked seriously.

"I think so—at least part of it. What are you doing here, Perry?"

"Playing light in the window. We figured this would be the first place you'd come to when you got back—if you got back. You caused quite a commotion when you disappeared. Pilgrim and Dr. Solow knew you had to be in the Army compound, but they didn't know what to do about it. Whatever son of a bitch is in charge down there sealed the place off. He wouldn't even talk to Pilgrim on the phone."

"Where's Sharon?"

"Up in the hospital with Pilgrim. He's been shot."

Veil tensed. "Bad?"

"Bad, but he's alive. At least he was alive the last time I called, which was fifteen minutes ago. The surgeons took a bullet out of his chest."

"Does anyone know who shot him?"

"No. Pilgrim is still unconscious."

Tompkins sprang to his feet as Veil headed for the door. "Veil! Before you go up there, let me get you some dry clothes! You're freezing to death!"

"No time, Perry."

"I'm coming with you!"

"No," Veil said firmly. "I have something else for you to do. I want you to round up all the people in the chalets, patients and Lazarus People, and get them someplace safe."

"What? Why?"

"I'm not sure why. I just have a bad feeling, Perry."

"Where can I take them? It would take hours to get them all across to the other mountain."

"No! I don't want them over there."

"Then where do I put them, Veil?"

Veil shook his head in frustration. "I don't know. Just tell everyone to be on the alert for anything unusual; I want everyone to be careful. Don't give a reason. I don't *know* the reason."

"There isn't anyone's feelings I'd trust more, my friend—and I do consider you my friend. I'll do what I can."

Veil nodded, then turned and hurried out of the office. He ran up the steep trail leading to the hospital, grew dizzy, and staggered the last fifty yards. He half fell through the swinging doors at the entrance—into Sharon Solow's arms.

"Veil, oh, Veil," Sharon murmured, cradling his head, kissing his eyes, his cheeks, his mouth. "When Perry called . . . I thought you were dead."

He had to get up, Veil thought as he fought against a furry darkness that threatened to envelope him, had to somehow keep going. His enemy was on the loose, and that enemy was unpredictable as well as deadly. There was no time to rest now.

But he couldn't take his arms from around the woman, couldn't take his lips away from the sweet-smelling, wheat-colored hair that fell across his face. He had been afraid that he was going to die without ever having told her that he loved her. Yet he couldn't tell her now; he could only hold on.

And drift away.

But not far away. He could not afford to pass out, he thought, even as his vision blurred and he experienced a nauseous, spinning sensation. He felt as if he were paralyzed, lying in a dark room where disembodied hands stripped him of his clothes, then wrapped him in something warm. There were voices—some near, some far away—but he could not understand what they were saying. Once, lips that he knew were Sharon's kissed him lightly on the mouth. More than anything else he longed to sleep, but he constantly fought to stay awake. There was so little time left; perhaps none at all.

If only he could see; if only someone would turn on the lights, open a window in the room, speak to him slowly so that he could understand. . . .

"You're incredible," Sharon said.

Veil jerked his eyes open, started to roll over, and almost fell off the hospital gurney. He sat up and swung his legs over the edge, then slumped forward as he experienced another attack of nausea and dizziness. Sharon steadied him, wrapping her arms tightly around his waist and resting her head on his chest. His wet clothes had been stripped from him and taken away, and he was dressed in a warm blue sweat suit. His feet were bare.

"How long have I been out?" Veil murmured as he clung to Sharon, running his fingers through her hair and kissing her scalp.

"All of an hour and a half. And you haven't really been out; you've been fighting it all along. You must think you're King Kong; no, you *are* King Kong. You've been dehydrated, sunburned to a well-done turn, and a blood test showed traces of what must have been a ton of some strange combination of amphetamines. God knows what you've been through, Veil, and you're still on your feet—or trying to get there." She paused, squeezed him. "The doctors wanted to give you something to knock you out. I said no."

"Thank you."

"I know you have things you must do."

"Yes."

"Veil . . . Veil, I was so afraid you were dead."

Veil gently pushed the woman away, then got down from the gurney. He swayed for a moment but steadied himself. Sharon came back into his arms.

"And I was afraid I was going to die," Veil replied softly. "I wondered why, because I'd never been afraid of death before. Then I realized that, until I met you, I'd never really understood all that life could be. *You've* become life to me, Sharon. You're an adventure I wish to experience, a journey I want to take. That's why I was suddenly afraid to die."

"Taking life for granted ties our tongues, Veil, as well as our hands."

"Yes."

"You've certainly untied both my tongue and my hands."

Veil smiled, kissed her forehead. "So I've noticed."

"You once invited me to tango with you on the edge of time. I should have taken the time we had then."

"Everyone has to do things in his or her own time. To face death doesn't mean that living should be rushed."

"Will we dance when this is over?"

"Yes."

"I wish there were time now, Veil. There are things I want to say to you."

"And I to you. But there isn't time."

"Not even for explanations?"

"Especially not for explanations. I have to go to Jonathan."

"I know." Sharon sighed, buried her lips in his neck for a few seconds, then abruptly broke away and gripped his hand. "Come with me."

Pilgrim lay on a hospital bed in the Emergency Care Ward. A sheet covered him to the waist, and his chest was heavily bandaged. A tube led from a needle in his arm to a bottle of clear intravenous fluid suspended from a rack beside his bed. His color was good, his breathing regular, and on his face was an expression of quiet rapture.

"When did it happen?" Veil asked quietly.

"Early yesterday morning."

After he had escaped from the cage, Veil thought. "Here or on the other mountain?"

"The other mountain. He was working late in his office, probably trying to figure a way to get you out of the Army

176

compound. The gunman must have taken him by surprise. One of the security guards heard shots and went running. He found Jonathan on the floor."

Not quite by surprise, Veil thought. His enemy would be a crack shot. Pilgrim had undoubtedly heard a chiming sound inside his head, had just enough time to react and save himself from an instant kill. "Is he going to make it?"

Sharon frowned and absently brushed a strand of hair away from her eyes. Veil glanced at her, and for the first time saw past her stunning beauty to the fatigue that had soaked into her bones and was pulling at her flesh. "I don't know," she said in a hoarse whisper. "The doctors don't know. They say it's up to him."

A young orderly entered the room pushing a cart on which was a tray of food, a pot of steaming coffee, and a small paper cup with two pills in it, one purple and one blue. Veil tossed the pills across the room into a wastebasket, then poured himself coffee and drank it down. The hot liquid seared his mouth, but at the same time filled him with a warm, satisfying glow that pushed back his fatigue. It was the second most delicious drink he had ever tasted.

"I've seen a few wounded men," Veil said around a mouthful of steak and mashed potatoes. "Considering the fact that he took a bullet in the chest, Jonathan looks in fairly decent shape."

"He was lucky," Sharon replied in a tight voice. "The bullet missed his heart and lungs. It ricocheted around his rib cage and came to rest without nicking any vital organs."

Veil took another mouthful of steak and potatoes, washed the food down with a second cup of coffee. "And?"

"With a long rest and proper care, he would recover."

Veil detected the note of deep concern in Sharon's voice, turned to her. "*Would* recover?"

Sharon did not answer, and she would not meet his gaze.

"Is he still under anesthetic?"

"No. That wore off hours ago." Now she looked at Veil, and tears glistened in her silver-streaked eyes. "Veil, he just refuses to come back."

Veil pushed aside the cart and went to Pilgrim's bedside. His hand trembled slightly as he reached out and gently touched the other man's shoulder. "He's there, isn't he?"

"Yes," Sharon replied simply as she wheeled over a portable electroencephalograph and attached electrodes to Pilgrim's temples. She turned on the switch; instantly the spiked EEG pattern associated with the Lazarus Gate appeared on the green cathode tube monitor.

Veil swallowed hard, found that his mouth was dry. "Bring him back."

"I'm afraid to authorize any kind of treatment, Veil. Look at the lines; look how strong they are. Jonathan is actually controlling his own state of consciousness. We're sure that he could live if he wanted to; I believe he could also will himself to die. I'm afraid that if I try to pull him back, he'll simply let go. I won't take the chance."

"But why—?" Veil swallowed the rest of the question. He knew the answer, and he voiced it. "He's waiting for me, Sharon."

The woman nodded slowly. "I know. I was afraid to admit it to myself, but it's the only explanation."

"Send me to him."

"No!" Sharon said sharply, bitterness creeping into her voice. "Jonathan has no right to do this!"

"Send me to him."

"I can't!"

"I don't believe you."

"Jonathan brought you to the Institute because you'd been painting pictures of . . . whatever that place is where he's gone. Can't you get there yourself?"

"Sharon, I painted those pictures from dreams—and I'm not exactly sleepy at the moment. Even if I were, I'm not sure what would happen under stress. Also, even if I could reach that state of dream-consciousness, there's no guarantee that I'd end up where Jonathan is. I've never been tested, so we don't know what my EEG looks like when I'm in that dream state. Jonathan is at the Lazarus Gate. It seems I've only been beyond; I've never seen any gate of light, never flown through an ocean of blue. I need to go where *he* is, and the only way to do that is for you to manipulate my consciousness until my brain-wave pattern matches his. You told me it was theoretically possible."

"He's been in love with death ever since the plane crash. Now he wants you to love her too."

"That's not true. You sound jealous."

"If I lose you because of Jonathan's madness, I assure you that what I'll be feeling will be a little stronger than jealousy."

"He has something to tell—or show—me."

"Then let him come back and tell you!"

"He can't, or he won't. I have to go there."

"Now you sound as crazy as Jonathan! Don't you understand? You can't *go* to him! There is no place to *go*. All the Lazarus Gate represents is a nerve spasm, a bit of brain chemistry changes in an instant of time before death. The fact that Jonathan has found a way to freeze that instant doesn't change the fact that it's all an illusion. Two people can't occupy the same place, in either space or time."

"We won't know that unless I try to occupy the same place. This is what my invitation to the Institute was all about from the beginning. It's one of the reasons Jonathan insists that I come to him—or at least make the attempt."

"Veil, don't you understand that I'd virtually have to *kill* you?"

Suddenly Veil found himself laughing. He stepped forward, took Sharon in his arms, and hugged her. "Come on, Sharon. I'm half dead already. Sending me the rest of the way shouldn't be all that difficult. I really do have to see if it's possible to have a chat with Jonathan where he is. He won't have it any other way."

Sharon pushed him away with both hands, then slapped him hard. When there was no response except for a sudden, cold glint in his eyes, she slapped him again. When she went to hit him again, Veil grabbed her wrist and held it.

"*You* have no right, Veil! You have no right to ask me to kill you!"

"But I *am* asking you," he replied in a voice that had grown

179

as cold as his eyes. "But you won't be killing me. You'll be bringing me to a state *near* death. Then you can bring me back."

"There's no *guarantee*, Veil! It's never been done!"

"I'm not asking for a guarantee. How could you put me under to the necessary degree? Answer me!"

"Drugs, I suppose," Sharon answered in a small voice. She was unable to take her eyes away from Veil's. "Maybe with the right mix of anesthesia, something paralytic." Tears welled in her eyes, and she choked back a sob. "Veil, you seem so different. I'm afraid of you."

"What about the brain-wave pattern? How could it be manipulated? Answer me!"

"More drugs," Sharon whispered, "combined with low levels of electricity."

"And bringing me back?"

"High-voltage electric shock. Perhaps. Maybe, Veil."

"Can you do it yourself?"

Sharon quickly shook her head. "*No*, Veil. It's . . . so complicated. At the very least I need to consult with an anesthesiologist and a neurologist. Then I'll need—"

"No! You're lying. You're a physician, and you've studied the problem; you're probably the *only* person who's studied the problem from a medical viewpoint. I'm betting you've done detailed computer simulations of exactly this situation. I'm betting you know, at least in theory, exactly what mix of drugs and anesthesia to use, as well as the proper levels of electricity. Am I right?"

Sharon closed her eyes to shut Veil out, but she could not hold back the truth. "Yes . . . but *only* in theory. Veil, I can't understand why you want to do this thing."

"I've already explained—"

"It's a madman's explanation."

"I'm not asking you to agree, and I don't have any more time to waste."

Sharon took a deep breath, slowly exhaled it, and opened her eyes. "I won't do it," she said simply. "Jonathan *is* insane;

I understand that now. You're insane for wanting to try what amounts to a stupid *stunt* that could kill you, and I'd be insane if I agreed to help you. I'd also be a criminal. I study death, Veil; I don't cause it."

"So be it," Veil said, releasing his grip on Sharon's wrist, turning and heading for the door.

"Veil, where are you going?!"

He wheeled around in the doorway. His tone was calm, distant, and very cold. "You won't do it, fine. This is a hospital. I'll find somebody around here who will."

"There isn't anyone else."

"There isn't anyone else who can control it, but I'll damn well find somebody who'll put me close to death. You once said I was a dangerous man, and now you say that you're afraid of me. Well, I assure you that I can be downright terrifying if I have a mind to be. I'm going to stop the first person, man or woman, in a white coat I come to. I absolutely guarantee you that in fifteen seconds or less that person will be absolutely delighted to put me in a very deep coma. After that I'll just have to take my chances."

Tears streamed down Sharon's cheeks, dripped on the floor. She tried to speak but could only manage to sob and shake her head.

"Are you saying you'll do it?"

Another sob, then a trembling nod.

"Good," Veil said curtly as he walked back into the room and stabbed a finger in the direction of a telephone on Pilgrim's bedstand. "Get whatever you need. Put me at the Lazarus Gate for fifteen minutes. That's all I'm asking for. Then try to get me back." Veil paused and breathed a silent sigh of regret as Sharon turned her back on him and walked to the telephone. "I don't suppose there's any way to lock this room up?" he asked softly.

"No." Sharon's voice was strangely muffled, as if she were holding her hand over her mouth.

"Anybody with a gun?"

"Not that I know of. No."

He thought about asking if there were any personnel who

would act as guards, then decided that it would be unfair to both Sharon and the "guards," who would be ineffectual, in any case, against the threat he was afraid of. "All right, Sharon," he said evenly. "Let's do it."

Sharon, moving like an automaton, picked up the telephone receiver and dialed a number. As she spoke, Veil experienced a sudden, almost overwhelming, sense of loss. He'd had no choice but to act the way he had, he thought, not only to force Sharon to do his bidding, but to free her of guilt in the event he died as a result of that bidding. That realization did not make him feel any better, for he now felt there was an unbridgeable distance between himself and the woman he loved. Sharon was only a few feet across the room, but he had pushed her clear to the other, dark side of his life, and he feared he would never be able to call her back; even if he survived the attempt to reach the Lazarus Gate and Jonathan Pilgrim, he had erased their future time together. He doubted whether they would ever dance.

His words and actions had been necessary and could not be taken back, Veil thought as he settled himself down on the floor in a corner of the room. He crossed his ankles, rested his wrists on his knees, and let his chin drop down on his chest. Then he began to take deep, regular breaths. He knew that more words could not heal the rupture in trust and feeling he had just caused. Now there was nothing to do but wait for the necessary chemicals and apparatus to be brought, nothing to do in the meantime but meditate and search for a calm center in himself in preparation for a journey through no time and no space, around infinity, to the Lazarus Gate.

Chapter 25

Veil . . . ?

He is pure blue flight, a sensation unlike anything he has ever experienced before, awake or in dreams. He is surrounded by a brilliant, electric blue, he *is* the blue, and when he looks at his hands, he can see through them. He *is* his hands, for there is no differentiation of limbs, body, mind, and organs, as such. There are no fixed reference points, no sound, only the conviction that he is traveling at great speed. He is approaching death as Sharon manipulates his life processes through drugs and electricity.

As Veil continues to stare at his hand a pinpoint of light suddenly appears in the blue beyond the palm. He puts his hand to his eyes and the light arcs through him, flashing down his spinal cord. He explodes and is reassembled, floating weightless, before a shimmering white radiance that he knows is the Lazarus Gate. No longer flying, he senses that he can now move where he wants, as in his dreams, simply by willing it. He wishes to go through the Lazarus Gate, and he does so without hesitation. There is a flash of blinding light and a great, booming chime sound that he feels in his head, heart, stomach, and groin.

Jonathan Pilgrim, naked like Veil, sits in the middle of the infinitely long corridor, which is bounded by walls of swirling gray. The former astronaut throws back his head and laughs when he sees Veil. Pilgrim is whole; there is no wound in his chest, and his eye and hand have been restored to him.

They embrace, and the fluid warmth Veil feels flowing through him is at once intensely sensual but transcends sexuality, raw emotion that pierces to the core of their common humanity, an affirmation of all things that human beings, male and female, share. It is pure love. They kiss, then step apart.

"How about that, sports fans?" Pilgrim says with a broad grin. "Some ride, huh?"

"Indeed," Veil replies, bursting into laughter that erupts from his throat as a variety of chiming sounds that bounce off the surrounding walls and cascade down around them like sparks. "I've never taken that particular route, but I've been here before."

"Of course. Now you can understand why I got just a little bit excited when I saw the work that you and Perry were doing."

"Yes."

"I've been kind of hanging around here waiting for you to show up."

"I know. How do you control it?"

"Haven't got the slightest idea, my friend. It just seemed like a good idea, so I decided to do it. I guess second-time visitors accumulate a certain amount of long-term credit here, if you will. I feel like I can stay or go back, as I choose. I could have come back and told you about this place."

"I already knew about this place."

"Yes and no. You didn't know that two people could

actually be here together, and that those people could communicate."

"Neither did you."

"Ah, but I suspected from the beginning. If I'd tried to convince you back *there*, wherever *there* is, you'd have thought I was crazy—which you started to think, anyway, after our last conversation."

"So now I think we're both crazy."

"Ha!" Pilgrim shouts, producing a deep, satisfying chime sound that reverberates deep in Veil's belly. Then he suddenly grows serious, although he is still smiling. "Thank you for coming, Veil. Doesn't it feel *good*?"

"My guess is that you and I are pumping one hell of a load of endomorphins, Jonathan. We're drugging ourselves; it's kind of a farewell gift from life."

"Let *go* of that kind of negative thinking," Pilgrim says with a hint of annoyance. Suddenly he laughs again, leers mischievously, and wriggles his fingers in the air. "Wouldn't the Russians give something to know about this?"

"Any intelligence agency would."

"Absolute, stone telepathy with stereo music, a light show, and all in living color."

"*Almost* living, Jonathan. You have a tendency to forget that little problem."

Pilgrim, still leering and wriggling his fingers, continues as if he hasn't heard. "Can you imagine what the world's spy masters would want to do with this place?"

"Yes, I can. Jonathan—"

"They'd make up their little plots, then try to recruit Lazarus People as spies. Around the world would go the Lazarus People, at least in the spy masters' minds. The Lazarus People would work diligently, nine to five, all week at their nefarious little deeds, and then—*yes*!—all meet here on Saturday morning at 0500, Greenwich Mean Time, for a conference. I love it! Beats blind mail drops, huh?"

"Except that a person would have to be three-quarters dead in order to attend this conference. That's tough duty,

Jonathan. Also, this is one conference we don't know it's possible to walk away from."

"A piece of cake. Sharon's done dozens of computer simulations. She got you here, didn't she? She'll get you back."

"I'm definitely counting on it."

"Not to worry."

"What worries me is the fact that I don't even have a distant relative who remotely resembles a computer simulation."

"It wouldn't work," Pilgrim says, suddenly serious.

"Uh, what wouldn't work?"

"The espionage scenario I just outlined. Lazarus People don't care about spying, and they won't lend their efforts to anything that might harm another human being. They can't be manipulated, and they'll just jerk around anyone who tries. Unfortunately, people *would* try. This place would become an obsession to any 'outsider' who even suspected its existence."

"Yes," Veil replies simply, remembering the network of caves.

"Great harm would be caused. Any information having to do with near-death studies would be classified. Hospital records would be searched, Lazarus People rounded up. Idiots."

"Jonathan," Veil says evenly, "I've got a flash for you. I'm not convinced this is happening."

Pilgrim frowns. "What are you talking about? You're *experiencing* it. That's why I waited for you to come to me."

"I don't know what I'm experiencing. A rush of endomorphins from my brain as I approach death, yes; that accounts for the ecstasy we feel, and that all Lazarus People report. As for the rest, it could all be a hallucination. I expected, I *wanted*, to meet with you, and so my dying brain may be indulging itself in a little wish fulfillment. You could very well be a hallucination, and I may be talking—thinking— to myself. There's only one way to prove that this is really happening."

Pilgrim turns his back to Veil, and when he speaks, his tone is almost petulant. "You're too heavy, Veil. You and I share what may be the greatest discovery about humankind in the history of humankind, and all you can do is talk like a goddam lawyer. Or a detective. I don't care if you are a detective; it's unbecoming."

"I'm not a detective, Jonathan," Veil says with a sigh. "I'm a painter. You have no idea how tired I get of explaining that to people; it ranks right up there with trying to convince people that I'm not a CIA agent."

There is a long pause, then Pilgrim asks quietly, "How can I convince you that I exist, and that this is really happening?"

"Come back with me and we'll compare notes. We'll go into separate rooms and write down our detailed recollections of this conversation. You're a scientist, Jonathan; you know it's the only way."

Again there is a long pause, during which Veil waits patiently, staring at his friend's back.

"How's Sharon?" Pilgrim says at last.

"More than a little pissed at both of us."

"I can believe that." Suddenly Pilgrim turns back to Veil. He is grinning once again, but the expression seems forced. "Oh, I almost forgot. Don't you want to know who the fucker is who shot me?"

"I already know. Ibber."

Pilgrim raises his eyebrows slightly. "How do you know?"

"Process of elimination, to begin with, combined with accumulated circumstantial evidence and an important slip on Parker's part. The more I thought about it, the more it always came back to the fact that it was Ibber who did my initial background check. Now, a standard check by someone who was only an Institute investigator would have turned up nothing but the garbage that the Army and CIA had strewn about. Granted that a good investigator would have smelled the garbage—something Ibber dutifully reported to you because he couldn't discount the possibility that you could have baited a trap for him. But Ibber was much more than just an Institute investigator; he was KGB, and the KGB file on me certainly hadn't been tampered with at all. All the KGB saw in their file was Veil Kendry before the Fall. Whatever they'd heard about the breach between the CIA and me, they weren't willing to buy it. Red warning flags popped up all over the place."

"What about the similarity between your paintings and Perry Tompkins's?"

"Then you know Ibber was spying on the hospice, using Army personnel?"

"The thought occurred to me at about the time he was squeezing the trigger. I'm a bit slower than you are."

"I'm not sure Ibber or anyone else from the compound who was sneaking into the hospice ever saw Perry's paintings; if they did, they wouldn't know what to make of them. They may have checked out a few chalets, but I'm sure they were far more interested in Sharon's files and the computer data. Ibber probably figured that you'd grown suspicious, and I was being brought in, through contacts you might have with the CIA, to do some general housecleaning."

"Why didn't he have you killed in New York? Why wait until you got here?"

"I'm not sure. He may have been afraid that I was closely guarded, or he may simply have considered the Institute a safer, more controlled situation. Also, he may have wanted to size me up in person, see how I reacted to him."

"Have you told anyone else?"

"No."

"Why not?"

"Ibber will kill anyone who looks at him the wrong way. I have to handle him myself."

"Well, you're pretty damn vulnerable right now. You're taking one hell of a big chance, my friend."

"I'm counting on Ibber thinking that I'm still holed up somewhere over in the Army compound."

"What did Parker have to do with it?"

"He said that he wasn't going to let *you* in. Well, Ibber also had access to the compound—so why not mention Ibber?"

"Ah, yes. I told you Parker was a fuck-up."

"If I'm right, Ibber is a bit more than a KGB agent who managed to penetrate your Institute. I think he's a KGB agent who managed to become a high-ranking Army officer in charge of that entire military installation in the valley. I was certain Parker was reporting to someone, and that someone was faking phone calls and feeding phony information to Parker just to make sure Parker would end up letting me die. It had to be Ibber, which means that the U.S. Army has a very fat KGB mole sitting on its collective face."

"Do tell," Pilgrim says in a somewhat cryptic tone.

"Then again, there's more than one spook running around over there. Someone arranged to spring me—who, and why, I don't know."

"Do tell."

"I must say that you don't sound too surprised."

"Don't I?" Jonathan says with a smile. "Go ahead; I want to hear what else you've been up to."

Veil studies Pilgrim for a few moments, but Pilgrim merely stares back, the same enigmatic smile on his face. Finally Veil shrugs, continues. "After I'd roamed around over there for a while, I realized that the safest and fastest way out of the compound would still be through a gate that Parker opened for me. I was hoping that turning myself in after having escaped might finally get the man's attention. But by then Ibber had already shot Parker."

"Parker's dead?"

"Yes."

"Parker was a fool," Pilgrim says softly, "but I'm sorry to hear that he's a dead fool."

"It meant that Ibber was in a panic, and for good reason. It had to have taken years for the Russians to maneuver Ibber into a position where he was both a DIA operative and your chief researcher."

"Well, the Army will have to take primary responsibility for Ibber; they had him first. He was strongly recommended to me by some friends in the military. Now I realize that my friends were probably being pushed by the DIA, because the DIA wanted to have their own man in here. Who turns out to be a KGB agent. That's a big ho-ho-ho on them, isn't it?"

"My concern is making sure that Ibber doesn't get the last laugh, Jonathan."

"Actually, I've been more than a little suspicious of Henry for some time. When that Mamba tried to kill you the morning after you'd arrived here, I decided it was past time to do some serious checking into Henry's background; not easy, since I didn't want to tip off the military that I was suspicious, and then have them tip off Henry."

Veil nods. "With Parker dead, I figured that Ibber would come after you—and maybe Sharon—next. If I was caught and killed inside the compound, there was still a chance he could cover his tracks."

"Where's Ibber now?"

"I don't know. Either on his way to Moscow, if he thinks he's totally blown, or looking for me. I'm sorry I couldn't get back sooner; I'd have saved you some pain."

"Do I look like I'm in *pain*?"

"No. As a matter of fact, neither of us has probably ever felt better. I understand things a bit better after coming here the hard way. It's no wonder Lazarus People no longer fear death."

"Death is love."

"I understand, Jonathan."

"Yeah. Anyway, I'm glad Madison got off his ass and told his man to spring you from that cage."

Veil feels a sudden stiffening of his spine, as if a wire running through him has been tugged. "How did you know about the cage? And where did you get that name?"

"From you," Pilgrim says easily.

"No. I never mentioned the cage, and I never mentioned anyone named Madison."

"Orville Madison," Pilgrim announces with a certain smugness. "Once your controller, and now a big—and very hidden—man in the CIA's nasties department, third in the chain of command behind the Director of Operations. You can bet your ass that I started some tongues to wagging when I called Langley's listed number, asked for Madison by name, and outlined his connection to you."

The wire pulls even tighter. "Jonathan, *how*?"

"Still think this is an hallucination, my friend?"

"*How*?"

"You sent out a cry for help, and I heard you . . . probably something to do with this place and our affinity for each other, although I haven't given it a great deal of thought. Yesterday, the thing you wanted more than anything in the world—except for a drink of water—was for Parker to call Orville Madison and have Madison verify that you couldn't be a KGB agent. Parker wouldn't listen; I did."

"My God," Veil whispers as the wire suddenly goes slack.

Pilgrim chuckles. "A new wrinkle, huh? It seems that in certain situations, with certain people, you don't have to come to the conference room to use the telephone. I'll tell you that it impressed the shit out of *me*. Incidentally, I also picked up the name, Lester Bean, but I sensed that Madison was more important. He was CIA, and he was the man I went after."

"Did you actually talk to Madison?"

"After a time, yes. He didn't have much choice. When they tried to put me off, I told them I was going to tell all sorts of old but juicy Veil Kendry stories to *The New York Times*. Madison came on the line."

"What'd he say?"

"Not a whole hell of a lot. Mostly, he just listened. I described the situation here, and shared my suspicions about Henry. I told him the Army had you, you were close to dying, and you needed help. After I finished, he said he'd take care of it. He warned me never to mention the call or the conversation, and never to call him again for any reason. Then he hung up."

Veil pauses, thinking. "The telepathy works even away from here," he says at last.

"Yes and no. After all, what we're sharing is one hell of a lot more than telepathy—whatever that means. The message from you was a good deal less. It was like a distress call that only I could hear, something which made me consciously uneasy but which I couldn't grasp consciously. Just as one has to view your paintings out of the corner of the eye, I picked up on what you needed out of the corner of my mind—when I was momentarily distracted by something else. Also, as I mentioned, the fact that you and I have a very special affinity probably had something to do with it. Identical twins often sense what happens to each other; you and I are twins in a different way. For want of a better expression, I'd describe us as astral twins."

"Still, it means that Lazarus People may have very special potential that nobody, except you and I, is even aware of."

"Lazarus People, and weirdballs like you and Perry Tompkins—yes. But clues, like the fact that Lazarus People tend to recognize each other without a word being spoken, have always been there. What's new is what's happening between you and me right now, this incredible *oneness*. We're not only proving that this state of consciousness exists, but that it can be maintained for periods of time far beyond the brief flash that Lazarus People have with the near-death experience. We're also showing that the state can be entered into, and controlled, by scientific means. I'd always suspected it, and I *knew* it when I saw the paintings you and Perry were independently producing. You were the key, Veil, the one person I needed to prove it."

"We haven't proved anything, Jonathan. This could still be my hallucination."

"Your escape from that cage wasn't an illusion; neither is this."

"I could be making up both ends of this conversation."

"Do you really believe that?"

"No," Veil says after a pause. "I do believe this is happening. But we still haven't made it back."

"I told you it would be a piece of cake. How much time did you tell Sharon to give you before she pulls you back?"

"Fifteen minutes, but I find I have no way of relating the quaint notion of fifteen minutes to what's going on here."

"I know what you mean; we're thinking to each other, and thought is one hell of a lot faster than talk."

"How much does Sharon know?"

"Before you accepted my invitation to come to the Institute, there wasn't much to know that she wasn't an expert on. After all, near-death studies is her field. I'd been here only once before, at the time I crashed in my plane. You came here all the time, in dreams, and Perry . . . well, the images began to come to Perry when he started dying. I've shared a few of my general speculations with Sharon, but that's all. She's always believed that the sighting of the Lazarus Gate is attributable to trauma and brain chemistry run amok in some people. She's certainly interested in the aftereffects of the near-death experience in Lazarus People, but she believes it's strictly a psychological phenomenon. Of course, she's standing over us right now, worried as hell, but she's convinced that we're stone-unconscious."

"I'm not so sure," Veil says thoughtfully. "Seeing the Lazarus Gate pattern on the monitor next to your bed may have made a believer out of her." He pauses, laughs. "Also, you've got the silliest grin on your face I've ever seen."

Pilgrim grunts. "Do I? Well, you'll have some stories to tell Dr. Solow, won't you?"

"Ibber suspected big things, obviously," Veil says seriously.

"Oh, yes. I'm sure that the hospice and what Sharon was doing in near-death studies has been uppermost in Ibber's mind from the very first day he reported for work, and his bosses must have hit the ceiling when I wouldn't grant him access to the hospice. His job had no connection with what Sharon was doing, so he couldn't argue the matter. But he had to have been pissed. Monitoring near-death studies would have been his number-one priority."

"Why so?"

"Both the Russians and Americans have always been officially interested in parapsychology, which is a category near-death studies fits into. Our Navy at one time funded a study to see if it was possible to communicate telepathically with submarine crews. But the Americans have always been unenthusiastic dabblers compared with the Russians. The

American government has never shown the slightest interest in Sharon's work."

Once again Veil thinks of the marked caves in the mountain and the hundreds of man-hours, undoubtedly expended on Ibber's orders, it must have taken to find the route to the hospice. "The Russians are certainly interested."

"Sure they are."

"The Russians must have a near-death studies program of their own."

"If they do, they've kept it a secret. But they certainly have thousands of individuals who've had a near-death experience, and the changes that take place in what we call Lazarus People wouldn't have gone unnoticed. It's impossible to say what they make of it, or what they've done about it."

"Maybe they've already sent somebody through the Lazarus Gate—or two people at once, like us."

"I doubt it. We've interviewed Lazarus People from all over the world, and I'm the only person I know of who's actually gone *through* the gate, seen what's here, and then come back. Then there's you, with your dream-paintings. The Russians don't have you. Indeed, you may be absolutely unique—and you proved to be the necessary catalyst. You have to know— or strongly suspect—that something is there before you search for it, especially if the search carries a strong risk of death. I doubt that the Russians would have risked killing people just because some individuals reported seeing a portal of light and felt terrific about it."

"But the Russians must be interested in more than the changes; they *do* suspect there's something here."

"Obviously. Otherwise, Ibber would have been as disinterested as Parker. They want to know what the military or population-control applications may be. They're fools."

"Why fools, Jonathan? My guess is that this experience transcends time and distance; if someone else from anywhere in the world were to be sent through the Lazarus Gate at this moment, we'd have company. And communication here transcends language. We're communicating with pure thought, which we happen to hear as music. It seems to me that the espionage capabilities look pretty damn good."

Pilgrim laughs and shakes his head. "You still talk like a detective, and you still don't get it."

"Get what?"

"You're not a Lazarus Person, Veil, so you don't feel precisely what Lazarus People feel, and you don't know what they know. Still, I don't think that anyone has ever been able to control or manipulate you. Well, Lazarus People can't be manipulated, because this experience brands a message very deep into the heart and soul. The message is that we—all of humankind—are *one*, literally. Birth and death are parentheses around lives that should be as happy, full of meaningful challenge, and as free from pain as possible. That's all. Everything else is an illusion."

"War isn't an illusion, Jonathan. Neither are bullets, bombs, torture, and a few thousand other things I could mention, including bad guys like Henry Ibber."

"Those things aren't illusions, but the assumptions that lead to their creation and use are. You don't shoot off your foot because it's infected, and you don't shoot off your neighbor's foot because your foot is infected. A Lazarus Person—*any* Lazarus Person, of whatever race or nationality—understands that his neighbor's foot *is* his foot, and he won't cooperate in any activity that is hostile to other human beings. You don't accept that, do you?"

"I accept what you tell me about Lazarus People, because you should know," Veil replies evenly. "I don't agree with your thinking."

"You behave as if you do."

"No, I don't. That's *your* illusion, Jonathan. I leave people alone if they leave me—and the people I care for—alone, but I assure you that I will shoot Henry Ibber's ass dead if and when I find him. And I won't confuse his ass with mine."

Pilgrim shrugs. "As I said, you're unique. It amazes me that you've been here so many times, and yet you still don't feel the *oneness* of human beings."

"All my life I've felt alone, Jonathan. What I've discovered in the last few days is an intense friendship with you and Sharon, and with Perry Tompkins. But Ibber's not my friend, any more than his ass is my ass. You see every human as being a part of some single, great organism or entity; I see every human as being essentially alone. That's the difference in our viewpoints."

"So be it," Pilgrim says with a sigh. "Anyway, speaking of Ibber, whatever he and the Russians may have thought we were up to, or were afraid we were up to, he sure as hell got an earful at that meeting you called. For the first time, he understood how important you were to me—in a way he'd never suspected. He saw that you were a catalyst, understood that you were the key to all sorts of mysteries the Russians were trying to solve. And he'd almost knocked you off."

"I'm sorry about that meeting, Jonathan."

"What's to be sorry about?"

"It brought matters to a head, and it eventually got you shot."

"Ah, but you're here and we're having this little musical chat as a result of that meeting. Who knows if I'd ever have gotten you to cooperate with me if Ibber hadn't reached the wrong conclusions, jumped the gun, and sent his man after you? Unexpected events and disrupted plans can often provide their own rich rewards."

"Indeed," Veil says softly as he thinks of Sharon. Suddenly he feels sadness soaking into his ecstasy like a stain.

"After that meeting, Ibber was probably tempted to shoot himself for screwing up my plans, which he could have monitored. But it was too late, Now you *were* trying to flush him out, and he may have known that I was suspicious of him. We had ourselves one very nervous KGB operative; if, with you, I was able to put something important together that he couldn't monitor, it would be his own damn fault."

Veil nods. "So he became defensive; his attention shifted to making certain that you *couldn't* use me for whatever experiments you had in mind. The possibility of you making some kind of breakthrough that he didn't know about was an outcome he couldn't afford."

"That sounds right."

"It's why he was so anxious to have me die in the compound." Veil pauses and again feels his spine stiffen. "It's why he'll eventually come here, to the hospice, if he isn't on his way back to Moscow."

"Let's hope your fifteen minutes are up soon," Pilgrim says easily. His eyes are half closed now, and he seems unconcerned. "I know you're anxious to get back and tend to all your illusions."

"Yes."

It is some time before Pilgrim speaks again. His eyes remain half closed, and he appears sleepy. "If you already knew that Henry was the bad guy, as you put it, why did you come here?"

"To bring you back with me," Veil replies simply. "I thought you understood that."

Pilgrim opens his eyes, dreamily shakes his head. "No, Veil."

"Your wound is serious, but you'll live—if you want to."

"I know. But why bother? There are too many illusions back there."

"This is an illusion!" Veil snaps, his voice ringing out as deep chimes that echo in the gray, swirling mist of the walls. He takes a deep breath, continues more quietly. "It's just an instant before death, a moment you and I have managed to stretch out. Full of illusions or not, *life* is what being human is about, not this giddy bullshit. When your body dies, the lights here go out and you're gone. Then you'll be nothing, Jonathan; *nada*."

"We don't know that," Pilgrim says in a somewhat defensive tone.

"*Know* it, Jonathan. Believe it. Sharon's right; this experience is just a momentary painkiller to help some of us, and maybe all of us, along the way when the time comes to die. Your problem is that you got hooked. Don't throw your life away. Come back."

Pilgrim again closes his eyes, says nothing.

"You can fight it, Jonathan," Veil continues softly. "You

did it once before; you fought like no human being had ever fought before. My God, *nobody* had ever been this deep into death, beyond that flash of light, and returned. You did, because at that time you understood that life is all there is. Now I want you to use the same will and guts you had then. I understand that you wanted me here. Okay, I came; I'm here. Now let's stop horsing around and both get back to where we belong. Sharon has to bring me back, because she had to fill me full of shit to get me here. All you have to do is will yourself to wake up. Do it."

"You don't understand, Veil," Pilgrim says dreamily. "Here I'm a whole man. I have all my pieces, and I'm not half exhausted all the time. I'm *happy* here. Aren't you?"

"Sure—but then, I tend to be a happy drunk. The difference between you and me is that I know when I'm drunk."

"You were pretty damned impressed with this experience a short while ago," Pilgrim says. His voice, his music, is suddenly bitter. "Why are you belittling it now?"

"I'm not belittling it, Jonathan. I haven't forgotten that the only reason I'm alive right now is because my cry for help somehow echoed through this place to you. I find the experience profoundly moving. I'm just trying to get you to see *all* that it is—and isn't. Sharon and I have a better fix on this geography than you do."

"There's love here. And Peace." Pilgrim's voice has once again become distant and dreamy. His upper body sways back and forth, as if caught in a breeze only he can feel.

"Maybe that's because you're a loving, peaceful man, my friend. It might be different for other people."

"I'm *so* tired back there, Veil . . . I'm tired all the time."

"I understand. But if you stay here, you're going to end up *dead* tired, in the most literal sense. This is one nap that's going to last forever. Your work isn't finished; in fact, it's just begun."

"So . . . tired."

"Well, you'll have plenty of time to sleep when you wake up, in a matter of speaking. You've found the Lazarus Gate, found a way to go through it and—I sincerely hope—survive. Together we haven't even begun to explore the implications for humanity. This is certainly no time for you to retire."

"Your . . . work now."

"No way, Jonathan. Don't try to lay off your responsibility on me. I'm a painter, remember? In fact, I don't think I'll ever do another dream-painting, because I understand now that they're about death. There are other things I want to do, subjects that are about living." Veil pauses and smiles gently at the other man. "If you'll pardon another atrocious pun, I've learned enough about death in the past few days to last me a lifetime. Please come back with me."

Pilgrim does not return the smile. "Good-bye, Veil," he says softly, then abruptly turns and walks into the mist to Veil's left.

Although Veil now suspects that the walls that he has always feared to look at may actually *be* death, boundaries around a last thread—corridor—of existence, he now unhesitatingly turns and peers directly at the spot where Pilgrim has disappeared. Then he steps through.

Instantly he is assailed by chimes of every conceivable pitch and timbre, sounds that swirl within his head, chest, and stomach like the gray in the walls. This is not the music of speech; always, he thinks, these chimes have meant danger. He knows that he is in grave danger now, but it is impossible for him to make any emotional connection with the concept of danger; he can only sense and note it intellectually, for he is filled with ecstasy to the point where he is actually weeping with joy.

Around him is nothing but solid gray—except for Jonathan Pilgrim, who stands before Veil with his body glistening like dew at sunrise.

Both of them, Veil thinks, are but a glimpse out of the corner of the eye away from death.

"It's an ocean," Pilgrim says in a hoarse whisper that is filled with awe. "Everything in the universe exists in the ocean, but human beings are so *heavy* that we're powerless to do anything but spend our lives trudging along the bottom." He sobs with ecstasy. "Except in dreams and death."

"Jonathan, there's nothing here. Nothing." He will not yield to it.

"Only as we approach death do we begin to rise toward the surface. It's so sad, Veil. So sad."

Danger. Danger.

"Veil," Sharon whispers in his ear, "I love you."

Veil turns and finds Sharon, naked and unutterably beautiful, standing at his side.

Danger.

"It's so easy to say that here," the woman continues. "I love you, I love you."

Pilgrim begins to dance, whirl, and giggle. Veil will not yield to it. Sharon reaches for him, but Veil steps away a short distance.

"What's happened, Sharon? Why are you here?"

"What?" Sharon giggles. "Did you think I was going to let you two guys have all the fun? After all, you're walking around in *my* field; I'm a professional, and you two gentlemen are just dilettantes. I was back there watching the two of you with your matching grins and brain-wave patterns, and I just decided there was no way I was going to be left out."

Danger.

"How did you get here, Sharon?" He will not yield to the giddiness that pounds at his stomach, making him want to howl with laughter.

Sharon shrugs and again grabs for Veil, who again steps out of the way. "Henry's maintaining us," Sharon says, cocking her head and smiling coyly at Veil as she cups her breasts. "He came in a few minutes after I put you under; he said that Jonathan had given him a key to the cable car after the meeting, and he'd come over to check on Jonathan's condition. Everything's all right. Really. It turns out that the procedure can be simplified. I explained to Henry what was happening, and what I wanted him to do. He's a physician, so he's as qualified to run that equipment as I am. The anesthesia and drugs are being automatically monitored. All Henry has to do is read dials and flip a switch in five minutes." She pauses, spreads her arms out to her sides, throws her head back, and utters a shrieking laugh. "*Voilà!* Here I am, guys! What a *trip*!"

Veil turns to Pilgrim, who shrugs and flashes a broad grin. "Uh-oh," Pilgrim says, and giggles.

Definitely endomorphins, Veil thinks, painkilling chemicals a hundred times more powerful than morphine, naturally produced by the brain, coursing through their systems.

"Come to me, Veil," Sharon whispers. "Make love to me."

"You're a dead duck, buddy," Jonathan says, "so you may as well enjoy what's left of the ride and oblige the lady. Go for it."

Pilgrim is right, of course, Veil thinks. Ibber does not have to bring him back to find out what is happening, for the KGB agent now has all the data he needs to enable the Russians to duplicate the experiment. He is indeed one dead duck, probably with only a few moments of life left to him while Ibber double-checks the dial readings and drug mixtures, and perhaps runs some simple blood tests.

Then Ibber will take care of some other business. He will destroy all the files. He will destroy the hospice. He will destroy the people in the hospice.

There will be a lot of dead ducks flying through the Lazarus Gate on this day. But Veil doesn't care. With nothing else left to do, he has finally yielded.

Now Veil gives in to the laughter exploding through him, then steps toward, into, Sharon. Their minds and bodies meld into one entity that is sexual love; they writhe as one in a prolonged orgasm that Veil feels must go on forever, until Sharon begins to disintegrate

"Veil"—Sharon sighs in an agonized whisper—"I hurt."

Veil separates his mind from Sharon's, but continues to hold her in his arms as she sags. Her flesh is melting away, exposing bone that glows iridescent green, like something radioactive, sick.

"It's because you don't belong here," Veil says. All ecstasy and laughter is gone now, but he must still fight for control against a giddiness that has suddenly turned nauseating. "It's the reason some end up Lazarus People, but most don't. You shouldn't have joined us, Sharon; you can't survive here."

"Veil, I love you. The real reason I came was because I couldn't bear the thought of you dying without . . . I hurt a lot, Veil."

The disintegration of Sharon's flesh continues, and Veil knows that he will soon be holding nothing but a glowing skeleton. Then that, too, will disappear. Desperately, he looks around him, finds Jonathan standing close by, wide-eyed now with horror.

"Jonathan! What can I do?!"

Pilgrim shakes his head. "I don't know, Veil."

"Veil," Sharon whispers, "it hurts too much. I think I'm . . . going to go away now."

"No!" Instinctively, Veil holds Sharon even tighter to him, then wills energy to flow from him into her.

Slowly, Sharon's body begins to form again, even as Veil begins to feel himself growing weary. And he is in pain.

"Sharon, *concentrate*," Veil continues. "You have to hang on; hang on to me. Don't think about anything else but our love, and don't move. Stay just as you are."

"Yes," Sharon answers dreamily. "I want to stay like this forever. With you, Veil, my darling. I don't hurt anymore. Do you?"

"No," Veil lies.

"Don't let go of me."

"I won't." He must fight now to keep his eyes open, and he wonders if his own flesh is melting away as he feeds his life to Sharon. He turns to Pilgrim. "Jonathan, are you all right?"

"Yes," Pilgrim answers in a hollow voice.

"She can't survive here. Do you understand that?"

"Yes."

"Then help me."

"I don't know how."

"*Think*, goddam it! I don't know what that fuck Ibber is up to right now, but Sharon is going to die unless he pulls her back!"

"The three of us are going to die, anyway, Veil. You know it. Ibber isn't going to pull anybody back."

"But he hasn't killed us yet! I'm losing it, Jonathan. I'm going to die soon, no matter what Ibber does or doesn't do. When I die, Sharon's going to die—and she's going to be in a great deal of pain. You have to go back. I know you have a chest wound; I know that you're going to be in a great deal of pain. But if you'll just wake up and reach for that switch, you can—"

"No, I can't," Pilgrim replies woodenly. "I already thought of that and I tried. Ibber understands; he has me hooked up with the two of you, and he controls me just as much as he controls you. I'm sorry."

As Veil has been speaking to Jonathan, Sharon's flesh has again begun to melt. "Sharon, I love you," Veil says, squeezing her. "You're letting go. Don't. I can't hang on to you if you don't want me to."

"You're . . . dying because of me; you're taking my pain. I feel it. I'm going away now."

"Sharon!"

"Call Perry," Pilgrim says abruptly.

Veil, exhausted as he channels more energy into Sharon's life, can only shake his head and mumble, "Can't hear . . . don't understand."

Pilgrim moves closer and shouts in Veil's ear. "Call Tompkins!"

"What? *Call* him?"

"Whatever you did when you were in the cage and got through to me, do that with Perry. The two of you have an affinity."

"Jonathan, I don't *know* what I did!"

"Well, do *something*! Think *at* him; focus your thoughts on him. Get him to come to the hospital."

"Ibber will kill him."

"Ibber's distracted right now. Besides, you forget; Tompkins is dying, anyway. He would consider it an honor and privilege to sacrifice his life for you and Sharon."

"He'll just get himself killed. Ibber's not the kind of man you sneak up on."

"All Perry has to do is get to that switch and send the recovery shocks through the two of you. Then it will be up to you, Veil."

"Veil, I have to go," Sharon whispers. "You're hurting so much . . . I feel your pain."

Veil shakes his head, torn by conflicting needs and desires. "Jonathan, God knows what kind of shape I'll be in when I come out of this!"

"I don't care what kind of shape you're in, my friend; I'll still put my money on you. It's the only way I can think of to save the two of you."

"But I can't ask—!"

Suddenly a light as bright as the Lazarus Gate appears to their left. It throbs like a breathing thing at its white-hot center, burning a hole through the death-gray.

"Veil—!"

"I see it!"

"Take Sharon and go!"

Holding Sharon tightly to him, Veil focuses all his will and energy on moving toward the light. Then Sharon's flesh begins to melt. He channels energy into her, but then feels himself slowing. For a fleeting moment, battered by desperation and exhaustion, he wants only to close his eyes and sleep. Die.

"Veil?" Sharon is smiling up at him. "Let me go."

"No! We're all going through. Hang on, Sharon. Concentrate!" He struggles toward the throbbing light, but his legs will barely support him. He feels as if he is sinking into a mire as deep as eternity. All of his strength is being drained by Sharon. "Jonathan! Help me!"

But Pilgrim has already come up behind him. He wraps his arms around both Veil and Sharon, and pushes them forward.

As they approach the gate, Veil hears the high-pitched hum of electricity. Now he sucks in a deep breath, tenses, leaps headfirst toward the blinding core of the light.

Pilgrim's hands release their grip on him.

"Jonathan!"

"Good-bye, Veil." Pilgrim's voice sounds as if it is echoing across a great distance. "Good luck. You don't need a half man with one eye, a hook for a hand, and a bullet hole in his chest."

Holding Sharon to his chest, Veil slowly tumbles through the gray toward the light. "Jonathan! We need you!"

"Good-bye, my friend."

Veil enters the light. Electricity crackles and dances over his flesh, pierces his brain and shakes his bones; the current becomes a knife slicing across his soul, tugging at Sharon, separating them.

He cannot hold on. Sharon is slipping away from him, being taken.

Veil twists through his pain, reaches back, and desperately gropes in the electric-white. But Sharon is gone. He throws back his head and screams with rage, frustration, and loss. He claws at the place in his heart where Sharon had been only a moment before.

Then he collides painfully with a hard surface that he knows must be.

Chapter 26

The floor of the hospital room.

Veil struggled to his hands and knees, then tried to stand. The room spun around him, and he crumpled back to his knees. He leaned on his thighs and shook his head, trying to clear it. His mouth was dry and filled with a strong medicinal taste. His forearms stung where needles had been torn from his flesh.

Some recovery, he thought.

Sounds of struggle came from somewhere across the room, slightly to his left. Veil lurched to his feet, staggered backward, and came up hard against a hospital gurney. His vision cleared slightly, and he found himself leaning over the empty gurney where he had lain. Parallel to it was the bed on which Pilgrim lay. Pilgrim was still unconscious, but his smile of rapture was gone. At the head of the bed was another gurney holding Sharon's still body.

Twenty feet away, Ibber and Perry Tompkins were rolling on the floor, their legs wrapped around one another as they struggled for control of a set of electric paddles connected to a portable emergency cardiac unit. Perry was losing; Ibber had the angle and was pressing the paddles inexorably closer to the sides of Perry Tompkins's head as the painter struggled to keep the other man's hands apart; veins popped and writhed in Perry's blood-flushed neck and forehead.

"Gun!" Tompkins gasped through clenched teeth. "On the floor under the bed!"

Veil started to lean over and almost passed out. Even if he managed to find the gun, he thought, there was no certainty that he could control his vision and movements well enough to aim it properly. Besides, there was no time; the live paddles were now barely an inch away from Perry's temples, and the artist appeared close to the point of physical collapse. When the steel paddles touched Perry's temples, Ibber would press the red buttons on their handles and send a deadly current through the other man's brain.

Veil pushed off the gurney, reeled across the room, and fell across the cardiac unit. He grabbed the heavy cables connected to the paddles and yanked. Flames arced, and sparks flew from the empty sockets, but the rubber insulation on the cables protected Veil from electric shock. He wrapped the ends of the cables around his wrists and yanked again, hoping to catch Ibber off balance. But Veil had no strength. Ibber, who had already pulled away from Perry's grasp, yanked back on the cables, pulling them away from Veil. Then he hit Perry on top of the head with one of the paddles, knocking the other man unconscious.

Veil swayed, partially supporting himself by leaning on the unsteady cart as Ibber, whirling the paddles by their cables like bolos, advanced on him. Suddenly Veil lunged forward, ducked under the paddles, and drove his forehead into Ibber's chest. Ibber grunted with surprise and fell backward as Veil wrapped his arms around the man's waist and fell with him, hoping to pin Ibber until more of the anesthesia passed out of his system and his strength returned, or until help arrived.

Ibber's fists pounded against the back of his head and neck, and into his kidneys; Ibber twisted one way, then another, until finally Veil's grip was broken. Ibber pushed Veil off and away from him, then rose to his feet. Veil, desperate to prevent Ibber from getting to the gun under the bed, clutched at the man's ankle.

But Ibber was not even going to bother searching for the gun; he didn't need it. The KGB agent disdainfully pulled his ankle out of Veil's grasp, then settled himself down on Veil's chest and reached out for the exposed throat before him. Veil barely managed to raise his own hands in time to momentarily shield his windpipe; it was a hopeless, desperate move, leaving him vulnerable to a dozen other deadly strikes, but he had no other alternative.

Ibber, however, seemed content to strangle Veil. Sweat glistened on the man's high forehead and in the hairs of his mustache, but his eyes were cold as he methodically pried Veil's locked fingers apart, then reached under the palms and wrapped the fingers of his right hand around Veil's throat.

Veil caught a movement out of the corner of his eye, over Ibber's left shoulder, and he shifted his gaze in that direction.

Pilgrim's body was twitching. The twitching stopped, and a moment later Pilgrim abruptly sat up in bed and clutched at his chest.

Ibber slowly tightened his grip on Veil's throat. Veil bucked beneath the other man's body, but Ibber had him firmly pinned. He could no longer breathe, and his own fingers were growing numb. He clawed at Ibber's hands, but the pressure on his windpipe steadily increased.

Pilgrim shook his head, then tore the needles out of his arms and looked around. His eyes met Veil's.

Veil wanted to shout, "*No, you'll hemorrhage!*" But no sound would come from his blocked throat. Shimmering red stripes were beginning to flash across his field of vision.

Pilgrim swung his legs over the side of the bed, hesitated just a moment to suck in a deep breath, then lowered himself to the floor and began walking unsteadily toward them. A red blotch had appeared on the bandage across his chest, and he walked slumped forward.

The red stripes were growing broader, then breaking up into black and gray dots that danced before Veil's eyes.

Pilgrim was only a few feet away when he stumbled. He caught himself, then coughed spasmodically. A red mist spurted from his mouth and nose, and the blood soaking the bandage suddenly blossomed like some malignant flower.

Ibber, startled, released his grip on Veil's throat and twisted around. He saw Pilgrim and immediately started to spring to his feet. Pilgrim coughed another spray of blood, then raised the hook that was his hand into the air and fell forward. Ibber's fist slammed into Pilgrim's chest at the same time as Pilgrim's hook penetrated the other man's skull and buried itself in the brain with a soft, curiously oral sound, like a *tsk*.

Then Veil lost consciousness.

He awoke to the feel of something cold and wet over his eyes. Veil swiped the ice pack away and started to sit up, but he was restrained by the strong arms of Perry Tompkins. He sighed, then lay back on the pillow someone had placed under his head. He was still on the floor.

"Easy, Veil, easy," Perry said soothingly. "The doctor who looked at you said you'd just passed out, but let's wait a few minutes to make sure that's all it is before you start moving around. The way you were flopping around on that cart—"

"Are *you* all right, Perry?"

"Yeah. I've got a hard head. In fact, I'm surprised that son of a bitch was able to knock me out."

"What doctor?"

"Dr. Dries. This is a pretty small shop, really not much more than a clinic, so most of the time there's just a skeleton crew of nurses and orderlies on the floors. The doctors have their own sleeping quarters in chalets at the back. I had to get Dries out of bed. Anyway, he's gone to try to call the State Police. He's not going to get very far, because all the phone lines have been cut. I tried to tell him that, but he insisted on seeing for himself. He'll be back in a few minutes."

"How long have I been out?"

Perry glanced at his watch. "About half an hour from the time I came around; I don't know how long before that."

Veil grunted and sat up. "I'm all right now. I guess all I needed was a nap. The anes—" Suddenly he remembered, and he gripped Perry's massive forearms. "Jonathan—?"

Perry bowed his head, then straightened up and moved to one side so that Veil could see the two sheet-draped bodies on the floor a few feet away. Both sheets were soaked with blood—one at the head, the other over the torso.

"He's dead, Veil," Perry said softly. "Hemorrhage; he bled to death. He did manage to put a very neat hole in Ibber's head before he died, though."

"I know," Veil said distantly. "It happened just before I passed out."

Veil extended his hand and let Perry pull him to his feet. He paused for a few moments to stand over Pilgrim's body, shook his head in sorrow, then walked over to the gurney where Sharon lay. The woman was absolutely still, an expression on her face of rapture, expectation—and longing. She did not seem to be in pain.

"Veil . . . ?"

"It's a long story," Veil said as he reached over Sharon's gurney and picked up the electroencephalograph electrodes that had been attached to Pilgrim's scalp. "You say the phone lines have been cut?"

"Yes."

"Where are the residents?"

"I rousted them out of bed and sent them into the woods. I didn't know what else to do with them."

Veil carefully placed the electrodes on Sharon's forehead and temples, the way she had placed them on him. "They're still there?"

"As far as I know, although by now some of them may have gone back to their chalets. I just told them it was an emergency. I was trying to move one Lazarus Person along when I got this terrible feeling that something was wrong at the hospital . . . and that you were in trouble and needed me. It's hard to describe just how strong that feeling was. I pushed the guy toward the woods, then came running up here. I'm not even sure how I knew to come to this room, but I did. Dr. Ibber was standing over the three of you. Well, Ibber has no business here at the hospice, and I knew that was what was wrong. A switch on one of the monitoring machines had a piece of red tape over it. Again without understanding why, I had this overpowering feeling that I had to get to that switch and throw it—after I took care of Ibber."

Veil flicked the control switch on the EEG unit. Instantly, the Lazarus Gate pattern, pronounced and steady, appeared on the cathode tube monitor. Veil sighed, reached out, and gently caressed Sharon's hair. "Ibber was a KGB agent, Perry," he said quietly, staring down at Sharon's still figure. "He was not only spying on the Army, but on Dr. Solow's projects as well. He shot Jonathan, and he would have killed all three of us if it hadn't been for you. I'm surprised he didn't manage to kill you."

Veil felt Tompkins come up beside him; a massive arm was laid across his shoulders. "He would have if it hadn't been for you. You came out of whatever state you were in like a drunk looking for a bar at closing time."

"Like a drunk, all right," Veil replied with a thin smile. "When you walked into the room, Ibber wasn't exactly eager for company."

"But Ibber wasn't you, my friend. Sick or not, I can still take care of myself pretty well. He started to pull a gun on me, but by then I was already across the room and putting my fist in his face. I—"

"Excuse me," a man in a white lab coat with a stethoscope around his neck said curtly as he pushed Veil aside and reached for the controls on the machines monitoring Sharon's life systems. "You mustn't touch anything."

Veil's hand flicked out, and his fingers gripped the doctor's wrist a fraction of a second before the man's fingers would have touched the controls. The viselike grip held firm as the man wheeled on Veil, dark brown eyes flashing. "Get your hand off me! Who are you?!"

"You know anything about the Lazarus Project?" Veil nodded toward the flickering white lines on the green-tinted screen above Sharon's gurney. "Do you know what that means?"

"Well, I . . ." The man's eyes said that he didn't.

"You don't," Veil said evenly. "In that case, I'm the man who's going to kill you if you, or any of your colleagues touch these machines or this woman before I say you can. You and I have a lot of research to do before anything's done with Dr. Solow. If she starts to fade, then treat her as you see fit—but as long as she's breathing steady and that EEG pattern remains like it is, you do nothing. Understand?"

"Dr. Dries, meet Mr. Veil Kendry," Perry announced wryly. "Doctor, Mr. Kendry is not a man to make idle threats. Unless you want your neck snapped, I'd keep your hands off Dr. Solow and the machines."

Dries shifted his gaze toward the dials, then again glared at Veil. "She seems stable now. You and I will talk later, Mr. Kendry."

"Fine," Veil replied easily as he released his grip on the man's wrist. Dries walked stiffly across the room to supervise two orderlies who had appeared with clean sheets and plastic to cover the bodies on the floor.

"What is that on the screen?" Perry asked. "I know it's an EEG pattern, but what else is it?"

"It's a kind of signature associated with a particular—and very special—state of consciousness."

"It has something to do with the paintings, doesn't it?"

"Yes."

"You've been *there*, haven't you? The three of you?"

"Yes."

"My God," Perry whispered.

"It's a place of wonder and horror," Veil said distantly. "I'll tell you about it when we have more time."

"How long do you want the Lazarus People and patients to stay hidden?"

"At least until I can take the cable car across to the other mountain and make some calls—assuming those phone lines haven't been cut."

"The police?"

"Police, hell. I want the Army up here."

"Why, Veil? Ibber's dead."

"I still have a bad feeling, Perry. In a short while it will be dawn. Ibber was on the loose, whereabouts unknown, for hours before he showed up here. I'm worried about what calls he may have made before he cut the phone lines."

"All right," Perry replied tersely. "You're the boss. I'm going back down and play sheepdog. Lazarus People don't take orders well, you know."

"Just a minute," Veil said, touching Perry's arm as he continued to stare down at Sharon's face. "Tell me exactly what happened when you threw that switch."

"I don't know *exactly*, Veil. I was slightly busy with Ibber."

"Tell me what you can remember."

"It was easy to see what was happening with you, even with Ibber all over me. You went crazy the moment I flipped the switch. You started flopping around like a fish. In fact, you flopped so hard that you went off the cart and fell on the goddam floor. On your head, I might add." Perry paused and smiled. "I was afraid you'd cracked your skull—which would have pissed me off mightily, considering the aggravation I was going through to save your ass from whatever trouble your ass was in."

Veil gently squeezed Perry's forearm. "What about Jonathan and Sharon?"

"As far as I could tell, Colonel Pilgrim hardly moved at all. Oh, he stiffened a little when the current went through him, but that was all. Dr. Solow first started flopping around like you were, as if she were struggling. Then she stopped. I think I saw her reach out her arm, as if she were groping for something. Then the arm fell back, and she was still—just like you see her now." Perry swallowed hard. When he spoke again, there was a slight tremor in his voice. "She's trapped there, isn't she?"

"I'm afraid so," Veil replied softly. The muscles in his jaw felt painfully stiff.

"But you woke up right away. Colonel Pilgrim—"

"I came back because it was what I desperately wanted to do. Jonathan came back *when* he wanted to, because he sensed—like you—that I needed help. I don't think Dr. Solow can get back."

"Is there anything the doctors can do?"

"That's what we're going to find—"

The explosion came from somewhere down the side of the mountain, but its force was enough to shatter a window and knock plaster from the walls and ceiling of the hospital room. Veil spun around and was at the window looking down over the mountainside in four quick strides. Through the aperture he watched as a cloud of black smoke rose from the site where one of the chalets had been, smudging dawn. The acrid smell of gelignite wafted through the window. Satchel charges.

"Sappers!" Veil shouted as he wheeled around and ran back to Pilgrim's bed. He got down on his hands and knees and began searching under the bed for Ibber's gun. "The son of a bitch did it! He called in sappers! They must have climbed up the mountain from the seaward side. He figured he'd gotten all the information he needed, so he called in a team of sappers to destroy everything—and everyone."

Veil found the gun just as another explosion sent more plaster raining down on their heads. The weapon was an American-made 22-caliber pistol, an assassin's favorite, very effective at close range but virtually useless beyond twenty yards. Veil gripped the gun, straightened up.

Perry was already out of the room and running down the corridor leading to the main entrance. Veil caught up with him at the swinging doors, grabbed his shoulder, and roughly spun him around.

"You stay here, Perry! There's nothing you can do down there! You're the last line of defense for the people in the hospital! Tell everyone you can find to get out and run like hell for the woods!"

"What about Sharon? Should I carry her out?"

For a few moments Veil was paralyzed by agonizing indecision. Finally he spat out the word, "No. If she's disconnected from the machines supplying her with drugs and anesthesia, I'm afraid she'll die—or worse. I'll just have to stop them before they get up here. Don't argue, Perry! Stay here!"

Then Veil was out the doors and sprinting down the narrow, winding path leading to Sharon's offices and a cluster of chalets. To his surprise and chagrin, Perry suddenly appeared beside him.

"The best defense is a good offense," Perry managed to gasp as he pumped his arms and raced alongside Veil. "Dries and the orderlies will take care of the other business, and you certainly made it clear to Dries that he shouldn't touch Dr. Solow. Also, there's no way I could stop anybody who made it up there. You were just trying to protect me."

"Damn it, Tomp—!"

They rounded a sharp bend and saw a green-uniformed man running up the trail toward them. Two large and ominous, rectangle-shaped bundles slapped against his sides as he ran. He carried a Kalashnikov assault rifle.

On the run, there was no way he was going to go up against an automatic rifle with a .22 pistol, Veil thought as the man glanced up and saw them. Virtually without breaking stride, the commando snapped his rifle up to waist-high firing position.

"Veil?!"

"*Dive!*" Veil shouted, squeezing off a shot as he left his feet and hurtled through the air into the thick underbrush that lined the trail to his left.

Perry dove to the other side as the assault rifle chattered and sprayed bullets through the space where they had separated only an instant before.

Veil fell through the brush and landed on his side, his fall cushioned by the soft loam of the forest floor. He rolled, then twisted into position behind a tree trunk as more bullets shredded the underbrush. He waited until the firing stopped, then reached around the trunk and squeezed off a round. He

VEIL

was immediately answered by another burst of automatic rifle fire that shredded the bark of the trees on either side of him.

It was like pitting a peashooter against a cannon, Veil thought. And he only had four peas left.

When the shooting stopped again, Veil counted to five, then burst out from behind the tree and started to race up the mountain, darting between trees, running parallel to the trail, searching desperately for some spot where he could get a clear shot at the sapper. But he was slowed by the soft ground and underbrush, and he saw a flash of Kelly green on the trail. Outdistancing him.

Four bullets—four chances to stop the man. Veil stopped running, braced, and fired through the trees toward the trail. One bullet glanced off a tree, and the other three simply missed their unseen target.

The man was gone, Veil thought as, for the first time in his life, he understood the full depths of meaning in the word *despair*. All the commando had to do was run another few hundred yards, throw one satchel in the front and the other at the back, and his job was done; the force of the twin explosions would rip out the entire first floor, and the building would collapse in on itself. And there was no way that Veil could stop him.

But Perry Tompkins could.

The burly figure of the painter, sprinting at full speed, flashed by on the trail.

Veil tore through the clinging underbrush and out onto the path, then put his head down and raced after the two men. When he looked up, he found that he had not closed the distance between himself and Perry. However, Perry was now perhaps fifteen yards behind the weighted-down sapper, and gaining. Gasping for breath, Veil reached down to the deepest part of himself for more strength and speed—and he slowly began to gain on the artist.

Then the commando heard, or sensed, Perry behind him. He glanced back over his shoulder, saw Perry barely ten yards away.

Veil started to shout a warning, but it was too late. The

commando had stopped and was already pressing the trigger on his Kalashnikov as he swung it around. The bullets caught Perry in midair, ripping through his midsection and killing him instantly as he fell onto the commando. The man collapsed under the weight of Perry's body. He struggled to free himself, but by then Veil, his long hair swirling about his head in the morning breeze, was standing over him, staring down into his eyes like a blond-haired, blue-eyed angel of death.

Veil crushed the man's skull with a single, tremendously powerful kick to the temple. Then he picked up the rifle, slipped in a fresh magazine, and sprinted back down the trail.

Tears glistened in Veil's eyes for a moment, then were gone—chased by the force of his passage and his will. He hoped there would be time later for proper homage, meditation, and free-flowing tears, to the men who had sacrificed their lives to save his and Sharon's; for now, the only proper meditation was to wreak destruction upon those men who would destroy the hospice and the people in it.

There was another explosion that shook the ground. A burst of gunfire somewhere across the compound.

Explosions were for buildings, Veil thought as his lungs and the muscles in his legs began to burn. Bullets were for people.

When he was twenty yards from the end of the trail that emptied into a clearing ringed by chalets, Veil cut into the woods to his right in order to reach the rear of the nearest chalet. He threw his rifle up on the roof, then followed it by scrambling up a tree and swinging over on an overhanging limb. He picked up the rifle, then crawled up the sloping roof and peered over the top.

From his vantage point he could see the entire clearing and all of the chalets that ringed it. There were two sappers at the opposite end of the clearing, standing perhaps thirty yards apart, spraying gunfire into the surrounding woods. Veil aimed and squeezed off a shot that caught the man on the left between the shoulder blades. The second man reacted and started to run to his right, but Veil calmly tracked the man with his rifle and sprayed the area in front of him with bullets.

VEIL

The man ran into them, danced for a moment like a drunken puppet as the bullets ripped through him, then collapsed to the ground when Veil released the trigger.

Silence. The eye-watering smell of cordite.

Veil waited, watching and listening. There was no sound except for the sibilant whisper of the waterfall in the distance; no sign of any people.

There were only the chimes sounding in his head, behind his eyes, and they were growing increasingly louder.

Veil quickly looked behind him, but he could see no movement in the forest behind the chalet. When he looked back, the satchel charge—thrown from somewhere beneath the chalet's front eave—had already reached its apogee and was falling toward him.

The satchel would be dialed for short-fuse detonation, Veil thought as he rolled down the roof—perhaps as little as four or five seconds, just enough time to allow the commando who had thrown it to duck behind a neighboring chalet or into the woods.

He made it over the edge, but the concussion of the blast caught him in midair. It struck him like an iron fist, spinning him in the air and hurling him to the ground, breaking him. He did not lose consciousness, but his left arm was bent back under his body at an impossible angle, and he just had time to bring his right arm over his eyes to protect them from the debris, shards of glass and wood, that rained down on him.

When it was over, Veil was buried in the afterbirth of destruction. He was not in pain, but his entire body felt numb. He also felt remarkably detached and clearheaded as he waited. And waited.

Finally there came a kicking sound, accompanied by beats of pressure on the left side of his head. The kicking became scraping, and in a few moments he felt a rifle butt bump against his arm as dirt and scraps of wood were scraped away from his face and chest.

Chimes tolled behind his eyes.

Veil slowly removed his arm from his face and found himself squinting up into the cold, vaguely curious, and surprised face of a man in a green uniform. The man grunted, then casually lifted his rifle and pointed it at Veil's head. Then a hole suddenly appeared in the commando's forehead, and from it spewed bone chips, blood, and brain tissue that sprayed over Veil's face.

Thwop-thwop-thwop.

With its blood-gorged, unseeing eyes still open, the body of the sapper crumpled onto Veil's chest. Veil turned his head away and spat out the man's gore. And he waited.

Thwop-thwop-thwop.

Perhaps he was unconscious—or dead?—and dreaming, Veil thought. He seemed to be back in a jungle clearing in Laos, surrounded by Hmong tribesmen, waiting as a helicopter came in low over the treetops.

Thwop-thwop-thwop.

If he wasn't dead, Veil thought, he soon would be. The helicopter was coming to spirit him away to Valhalla.

Endomorphins.

Thwop-thwop-chiiiir.

There was a gust of wind that ruffled Veil's hair and the sapper's shirt. Then the motor died and there was silence surrounding him once again.

Or did he hear footsteps? It was hard for Veil to tell, for the sound of the explosion was still ringing in his ears.

A shoe sole appeared in his field of vision, coming from over his right shoulder. The sole moved on to reveal a dusty, wingtip shoe and brown wool slacks that clashed with blue argyle socks. The man who owned the shoe, slacks, and sock pushed the sapper's body off Veil.

"For chrissake, Kendry," Orville Madison said brusquely. "What a mess. I never thought I'd see the day when I had to play fucking nursemaid to you."

Chapter 27

Veil stared through the glass partition built into the wall of the Army hospital room at the still figure of Sharon, who was dressed in a lacy, blue nightgown Veil had bought for her. On a table next to her bed, bellows attached to an oxygen tent rose and fell in perfect, mindless rhythm. Needles slipped into her veins carried nourishment—and the Lazarus Gate drug mixture—into her system and carried away waste. Electrodes attached to her body recorded her heartbeat, as well as a brain-wave pattern that indicated to Veil that Sharon was still somewhere beyond the Lazarus Gate, wandering alone in the gray mist where he had lost her. On her face was the same expression of rapture and longing that Veil had seen in the hospital clinic.

"I haven't had a chance to thank you for bailing me out of the Army compound," Veil said in a flat voice. "I'm thanking you now."

Orville Madison grunted as he lit a cigar, ignoring the NO SMOKING sign posted in the small observers' gallery outside Sharon's room. "You know better than to thank me, Kendry. You're mine to kill, if and when I choose to, not the Army's. I was just protecting my prerogatives."

"Yeah? Well, I'm here to tell you that you shaved this particular prerogative pretty close. How the hell did you think I was going to get out of the compound itself?"

"Funny thing about that; there was never any doubt in my mind that you'd find a way. What's the matter? Age catching up with you?"

"As a matter of fact, yes. You don't look so hot yourself. You're even fatter than when I last saw you, and that stupid toupee you're wearing looks like shit."

"How did this Pilgrim fellow get my name?"

"It's a mystery."

Madison turned his head and squinted at Veil. "Is it?"

"Very much so."

"Pilgrim gave me some background on the phone, but I still need the answers to a lot of questions. Now that you're up and about, will you talk to me?"

Veil shifted his left arm to a more comfortable position in its sling. "What do you want to know?"

"What the *hell* was Ibber doing trying to blow up a hospice and blow away a bunch of ex-stiffs and future stiffs?"

"He didn't want anyone else to know what Jonathan and Sharon had discovered, and he couldn't be certain how many others did know. His solution was to kill everyone."

Madison puffed slowly on his cigar, feigning boredom and indifference, but the sudden tightness in his voice betrayed him. "What was it they discovered?"

"That there's a state of consciousness, a fleeting moment, some men and women experience as they approach death when minds merge."

"What the fuck are you talking about?"

"You want me to say it again?"

"I heard what you said; I want to know what you mean. It sounds like you're saying that dying people, if they're dead enough, can communicate with each other."

"You've got it. Except that the people doing the communicating have to be dying together, and they have to reach this precise state of consciousness at precisely the same time—or close to it."

"You're bullshitting me, Kendry."

With the aid of his cane Veil shuffled around until he was squarely facing the other men. "No. It's the truth, Madison. Now you know more than Ibber actually knew. He only suspected it, and that was enough to make him do what he did."

"There must be more."

"Ibber also suspected that you could stretch out, or freeze, that moment. He was right." Veil nodded toward the figure on the other side of the glass. "That's what happens."

Madison's eyes had narrowed to slits. "You're trying to tell me that a KGB agent who'd penetrated a top command post of the United States Army then proceeded to throw it all away because he wanted to start a vegetable patch?"

Veil winced inwardly; the other man hadn't changed. "He didn't know that would happen; nobody knew at the time Sharon attempted it. He just wanted to make certain that we couldn't use any of this information militarily."

"Is there any way we can use it militarily?"

"Ibber thought so."

"Do you think so?"

"No."

"Where can I get a second opinion?"

"Try the Russians."

"Come on, Kendry. You owe me."

Again, Veil nodded toward Sharon. "If she ever comes out of the coma, she'd be a good person to ask. Or you can talk to other scientists doing near-death research. Hell, have the CIA start its own hospice and see what you can find out."

"Why do I have the strong feeling that you're hiding something?"

"I don't know. Do I sound or act as if I'm hiding something?"

"No," Madison finally said after a long pause. "What were

you doing over in the Army compound in the first place? Pilgrim never got around to explaining that to me."

Veil smiled, then grimaced as the wires in his jaw cut into his gums. "You think I'm working for somebody?"

"Unless you've got a double, I know you're not. That doesn't answer my question."

"Ibber was afraid I might be working for you people—and that's no joke. He sent an assassin after me the morning after I arrived. I was over there trying to find out why."

Madison dropped his cigar on the floor and ground it out with the toe of his shoe. "Shit," he said dispassionately. "What a waste of time."

"Yeah."

"If I'd known this was all there was to it, I might have decided to let Ibber kill you."

"You were always a prince, Madison."

"Can you believe that I'm still pissed at you after all these years? I've got pins in both my collarbones, and they hurt like hell when it rains or snows. Also, I'd probably be top man in Operations if I hadn't lost four years making up the ground you'd shoveled out from under me."

"Madison," Veil said evenly, "I have a personal favor to ask of you."

"Do you, now. What is it?"

"I want you to take this woman out of here and put her in one of your facilities at Langley—under your absolute control and personal supervision. I'm sure she must have family, but I don't know who, or where, they are. Your people will take care of notification and make up some kind of story about why she has to be where she is. I want the absolute best for her—twice-daily massage, the works. I want her to keep looking beautiful."

"Is that all?" Madison asked, making no effort to mask his sarcasm.

"No, it isn't. You keep her in *exactly* the state she's in now, unless I say differently."

"Unless you say differently?"

"If I give the word, you see to it that somebody pulls the plug; you let her die—but only if I give the word."

Madison studied Veil for some time. "You still have a taste for playing God, don't you?" he said at last.

"I love her," Veil replied simply. "Also, I need time to think. In the meantime I have to know that her body, at least, is safe."

"What you're asking could end up costing the taxpayers of this nation a lot of bucks. Hell, we could keep her alive for years."

"You don't give a damn about the change in your pocket, what's more anything you do at taxpayers' expense."

"So what? Why should I do anything for you?"

"I want you to do it for the woman."

"Why should I do it for the woman?"

"Because Veil Kendry is humbling himself to ask you—and that has to give you one hell of a lot of personal satisfaction."

"It does, but that's not enough. The answer is no."

"I took care of Ibber for you. If it weren't for me, that bastard would still be sending our secrets back to Mother Russia."

"What do you want to do, close down the spy industry? Your kind of thinking could cost me my job."

"I answered your questions freely, told you what you wanted to know. I could have held out and I didn't."

"Big deal."

"Madison, for chrissake, you want me to beg? I'm begging. If I weren't stuck in all this plaster. I'd get down on my knees."

"That would be an amusing sight, but I have a better idea," Madison said casually as he lit a fresh cigar. He studied the flame at the end of the match as if there were some secret message in it. "Work for me."

"No."

"Take care of yourself, Kendry," Madison said, and blew out the match. Then he turned and headed down the corridor.

"Madison!" Veil waited as the man stopped, slowly turned. Then Veil nodded his head. It felt as if the back of his neck were being seared with a blowtorch, but he knew that the pain was only in his mind. "All right."

"What if you call me up tomorrow and tell me to kill her?"

"Our deal still stands; you own me. You have my word."

"I'll accept that any day."

"Special assignments only."

"Sure. Did you think I was going to send Veil Kendry out to make nasty faces at Castro?"

"I mean that I have approval over any assignment. If I don't like it, I don't do it."

"Jesus Christ, you *still* believe that there are good guys and bad guys, don't you?"

"Give it to me, Madison."

After a long pause Madison finally nodded and smiled. The smile didn't touch his eyes. "Why not? Far be it from me to ask you to do something you didn't approve of. Good grief."

"In the meantime I keep doing what I'm doing now. Except for when you want me."

"Oh, I insist; it's a great cover. Anything else?"

"No."

Madison laughed loudly. "*Damn*, Kendry, you are one hell of a negotiator. Thank God the State Department didn't get to you first." He casually waved his cigar in the direction of the room beyond the glass. "Don't worry about Sleeping Beauty. I'll have her safely tucked away in her new bedroom by dinnertime."

And all he had given away was his soul, Veil thought as he watched Madison, trailing blue smoke, disappear around a bend in the corridor. Finally Madison had what he had always wanted.

It had been quite a barter.

But then, Veil thought as he leaned his head against the glass, he had what *he* wanted. Already his entire attention was drifting to Sharon—now, quite literally, the woman of his dreams.

He was tired, ready to sleep.

Chapter 28

Veil dreams.

Vivid dreaming is his gift and affliction, the lash of memory and a guide to justice, a mystery and sometimes the key to mystery, prod to violence and maker of peace, an invitation to madness and the fountainhead of his power as an artist.

Now vivid dreaming is also his passport to the land where his love is lost. He searches, does not find her, and escapes from the mist the way he has always escaped from dreams, by rolling away. But he searches again and again, until in one dream he finally finds her, exactly as he left her, the process of disintegration halted by his unsuccessful attempt to bring her back along an electric road.

Together they reaffirm the truth that love and courage, while not antidotes to death, are the heart and spine of hope. They meet and talk many times—of their love, of the near-death experience, and of dreaming and escaping from dreams.

Then one dream, when all the mechanical things have been disconnected from her body, Sharon is able to allow Veil gently to lift her in the arms of his mind and roll her away with him. . . .

MORE MYSTERIOUS PLEASURES

HAROLD ADAMS
MURDER
Carl Wilcox debuts in a story of triple murder which exposes the underbelly of corruption in the town of Corden, shattering the respectability of its most dignified citizens.   #501 $3.50

THE NAKED LIAR
When a sexy young widow is framed for the murder of her husband, Carl Wilcox comes through to help her fight off cops and big-city goons.
                                                               #420 $3.95

THE FOURTH WIDOW
Ex-con/private eye Carl Wilcox is back, investigating the death of a "popular" widow in the Depression-era town of Corden, S.D.
                                                               #502 $3.50

EARL DERR BIGGERS
THE HOUSE WITHOUT A KEY
Charlie Chan debuts in the Honolulu investigation of an expatriate Bostonian's murder.   #421 $3.95

THE CHINESE PARROT
Charlie Chan works to find the key to murders seemingly without victims—but which have left a multitude of clues.   #503 $3.95

BEHIND THAT CURTAIN
Two murders sixteen years apart, one in London, one in San Francisco, each share a major clue in a pair of velvet Chinese slippers. Chan seeks the connection.   #504 $3.95

THE BLACK CAMEL
When movie goddess Sheila Fane is murdered in her Hawaiian pavilion, Chan discovers an interrelated crime in a murky Hollywood mystery from the past.   #505 $3.95

CHARLIE CHAN CARRIES ON
An elusive transcontinental killer dogs the heels of the Lofton Round the World Cruise. When the touring party reaches Honolulu, the murderer finally meets his match.   #506 $3.95

JOE GORES
A TIME OF PREDATORS
When Paula Halstead kills herself after witnessing a horrid crime, her husband vows to avenge her death. Winner of the Edgar Allan Poe Award. #215 $3.95

COME MORNING
Two million in diamonds are at stake, and the ex-con who knows their whereabouts may have trouble staying alive if he turns them up at the wrong moment. #518 $3.95

NAT HENTOFF
BLUES FOR CHARLIE DARWIN
Gritty, colorful Greenwich Village sets the scene for Noah Green and Sam McKibbon, two street-wise New York cops who are as at home in jazz clubs as they are at a homicide scene. #208 $3.95

THE MAN FROM INTERNAL AFFAIRS
Detective Noah Green wants to know who's stuffing corpses into East Village garbage cans . . . and who's lying about him to the Internal Affairs Division. #409 $3.95

PATRICIA HIGHSMITH
THE BLUNDERER
An unhappy husband attempts to kill his wife by applying the murderous methods of another man. When things go wrong, he pays a visit to the more successful killer—a dreadful error. #305 $3.95

DOUG HORNIG
THE DARK SIDE
Insurance detective Loren Swift is called to a rural commune to investigate a carbon-monoxide murder. Are the commune inhabitants as gentle as they seem? #519 $3.95

P.D. JAMES/T.A. CRITCHLEY
THE MAUL AND THE PEAR TREE
The noted mystery novelist teams up with a police historian to create a fascinating factual account of the 1811 Ratcliffe Highway murders. #520 $3.95

STUART KAMINSKY'S "TOBY PETERS" SERIES
NEVER CROSS A VAMPIRE
When Bela Lugosi receives a dead bat in the mail, Toby tries to catch the prankster. But Toby's time is at a premium because he's also trying to clear William Faulkner of a murder charge! #107 $3.95

HIGH MIDNIGHT
When Gary Cooper and Ernest Hemingway come to Toby for protection, he tries to save them from vicious blackmailers.   #106 $3.95

HE DONE HER WRONG
Someone has stolen Mae West's autobiography, and when she asks Toby to come up and see her sometime, he doesn't know how deadly a visit it could be.   #105 $3.95

BULLET FOR A STAR
Warner Brothers hires Toby Peters to clear the name of Errol Flynn, a blackmail victim with a penchant for young girls. The first novel in the acclaimed Hollywood-based private eye series.   #308 $3.95

THE FALA FACTOR
Toby comes to the rescue of lady-in-distress Eleanor Roosevelt, and must match wits with a right-wing fanatic who is scheming to overthrow the U.S. Government.   #309 $3.95

JOSEPH KOENIG
FLOATER
Florida Everglades sheriff Buck White matches wits with a Miami murder-and-larceny team who just may have hidden his ex-wife's corpse in a remote bayou.   #521 $3.50

ELMORE LEONARD
THE HUNTED
Long out of print, this 1974 novel by the author of *Glitz* details the attempts of a man to escape killers from his past.   #401 $3.95

MR. MAJESTYK
Sometimes bad guys can push a good man too far, and when that good guy is a Special Forces veteran, everyone had better duck.   #402 $3.95

THE BIG BOUNCE
Suspense and black comedy are cleverly combined in this tale of a dangerous drifter's affair with a beautiful woman out for kicks.   #403 $3.95

ELSA LEWIN
I, ANNA
A recently divorced woman commits murder to avenge her degradation at the hands of a sleazy lothario.   #522 $3.50

THOMAS MAXWELL
KISS ME ONCE
An epic *roman noir* which explores the romantic but seamy underworld of New York during the WWII years. When the good guys are off fighting in Europe, the bad guys run amok in America.   #523 $3.95

ED McBAIN

ANOTHER PART OF THE CITY
The master of the police procedural moves from the fictional 87th precinct to the gritty reality of Manhattan. "McBain's best in several years."—*San Francisco Chronicle*.   #524 $3.95

SNOW WHITE AND ROSE RED
A beautiful heiress confined to a sanitarium engages Matthew Hope to free her—and her $650,000.   #414 $3.95

CINDERELLA
A dead detective and a hot young hooker lead Matthew Hope into a multi-layered plot among Miami cocaine dealers. "A gem of sting and countersting."—*Time*.   #525 $3.95

PETER O'DONNELL

MODESTY BLAISE
Modesty and Willie Garvin must protect a shipment of diamonds from a gentleman about to murder his lover and an *uncivilized* sheik.   #216 $3.95

SABRE TOOTH
Modesty faces Willie's apparent betrayal and a modern-day Genghis Khan who wants her for his mercenary army.   #217 $3.95

A TASTE FOR DEATH
Modesty and Willie are pitted against a giant enemy in the Sahara, where their only hope of escape is a blind girl whose time is running out.   #218 $3.95

I, LUCIFER
Some people carry a nickname too far . . . like the maniac calling himself Lucifer. He's targeted 120 souls, and Modesty and Willie find they have a personal stake in stopping him.   #219 $3.95

THE IMPOSSIBLE VIRGIN
Modesty fights for her soul when she and Willie attempt to rescue an albino girl from the evil Brunel, who lusts after the secret power of an idol called the Impossible Virgin.   #220 $3.95

DEAD MAN'S HANDLE
Modesty Blaise must deal with a brainwashed—and deadly—Willie Garvin as well as with a host of outré religion-crazed villains.

#526 $3.95

ELIZABETH PETERS

CROCODILE ON THE SANDBANK
Amelia Peabody's trip to Egypt brings her face to face with an ancient mystery. With the help of Radcliffe Emerson, she uncovers a tomb and the solution to a deadly threat.   #209 $3.95

THE CURSE OF THE PHARAOHS
Amelia and Radcliffe Emerson head for Egypt to excavate a cursed tomb but must confront the burial ground's evil history before it claims them both.
#210 $3.95

THE SEVENTH SINNER
Murder in an ancient subterranean Roman temple sparks Jacqueline Kirby's first recorded case.
#411 $3.95

THE MURDERS OF RICHARD III
Death by archaic means haunts the costumed weekend get-together of a group of eccentric Ricardians.
#412 $3.95

ANTHONY PRICE
THE LABYRINTH MAKERS
Dr. David Audley does his job too well in his first documented case, embarrassing British Intelligence, the CIA, and the KGB in one swoop.
#404 $3.95

THE ALAMUT AMBUSH
Alamut, in Northern Persia, is considered by many to be the original home of terrorism. Audley moves to the Mideast to put the cap on an explosive threat.
#405 $3.95

COLONEL BUTLER'S WOLF
The Soviets are recruiting spies from among Oxford's best and brightest; it's up to Dr. Audley to identify the Russian wolf in don's clothing.
#527 $3.95

OCTOBER MEN
Dr. Audley's "holiday" in Rome stirs up old Intelligence feuds and echoes of partisan warfare during World War II—and leads him into new danger.
#529 $3.95

OTHER PATHS TO GLORY
What can a World War I battlefield in France have in common with a deadly secret of the present? A modern assault on Bouillet Wood leads to the answers.
#530 $3.95

SION CROSSING
What does the chairman of a new NATO-like committee have to do with the American Civil War? Audley travels to Georgia in this espionage thriller.
#406 $3.95

HERE BE MONSTERS
The assassination of an American veteran forces Dr. David Audley into a confrontation with undercover KGB agents.
#528 $3.95

BILL PRONZINI AND JOHN LUTZ
THE EYE
A lunatic watches over the residents of West 98th Street with a powerful telescope. When his "children" displease him, he is swift to mete out deadly punishment.
#408 $3.95

DAVID WILLIAMS' "MARK TREASURE" SERIES
UNHOLY WRIT
London financier Mark Treasure helps a friend reaquire some property. He stays to unravel the mystery when a Shakespeare manuscript is discovered and foul murder done. #112 $3.95

TREASURE BY DEGREES
Mark Treasure discovers there's nothing funny about a board game called "Funny Farms." When he becomes involved in the takeover struggle for a small university, he also finds there's nothing funny about murder. #113 $3.95
